Looking for
Lucie

by Ted Lamb

By the same author

Journalist Ted Lamb, 67, is author of print books The Penguin Book of Fishing, Penguin guides to sea and freshwater fishing in Britain, The Bait Book and Effective Media Coverage. Published on Amazon Kindle also are Brassribs - the story of a carp (and the first part of the Brightwell Trilogy, to which Looking for Lucie is the sequel); novels Gansalaman's Gold and Match of the Day; novelette The Box; and children's story Monty and the Mauler. Poetry works on Kindle are One Last Cast and The Ballad of Sally Stardust.

ISBN: 978-0-9575093-0-6

Published by Edict Editorial, Myrtle Cottage, Blakeney Hill Road, Blakeney, Glos GL15 4BT

Tel: 01594 510470.

Email: edictserv@yahoo.co.uk

For Sarah and Caspar

Thanks also to Anne Gordon for patient and constructive criticism.

Chapter 1

To anyone walking the loch-side road on this stormy late October day – and few would care to be out in such weather from choice - the lone fisherman in a tiny boat at one end of the heaving dark grey water will strike a forlorn figure. They might strain to even see him there amid the encroaching gloom, sinking and rising in the swell while a flock of gulls wheels wildly across the black sky. Soon, only the occasional glimpse of the white rim of his dinghy gives his presence away. It is inconceivable he is not scurrying for cover, especially with night rapidly approaching. Indeed, it would be reasonable to speculate that some misery in the man's home life is preventing him from watching telly by a cosy fireside - or maybe mental instability has driven him to this extreme.

What observers (if there are any) will not know is that the man is on a mission - a mission which only the keenest of fellow pike fisherman could possibly understand. But perhaps also he really is more than a little mad, impelled by this quest and ensnared by the notion that he might succeed where many others have failed - like people driven to hunt for the ever-elusive and for all anyone knows non-existent Holy Grail. He is, however, quite certain of the facts that guide his actions, facts that have brought him to this spot at this very time. He is looking for a fish, and though this is in all likelihood an old fish, it is not just any old fish...

His driving force: somewhere in the British Isles, he is convinced, there is without doubt a pike far heavier than the current record rod-caught fish, which is nearly 47 pounds. Perhaps it could even be a 60 pound-plus fish. There may be bigger pike still, he believes, and there may well be many more of these giants than is currently thought.

The fisherman would have you consider a few points before you dismiss such notions as far-fetched. In England, Wales and Ireland there are many thousands of square miles of water containing pike - it's a widespread species - and although pike fishing has a lot of enthusiastic fans, you could probably fit all of them together into the space of a 50-acre pool, boats, fishing tackle and all, with room to spare. It's hard to imagine the exact ratio of pike to anglers in all of Britain's H2O, but let's just say we are outnumbered to a high degree, and all our efforts combined would not enable one of us to drop a bait within a mile of a goodly number of bigger fish, let alone have a go at tempting the biggest pike in Britain.

A hopeless task, then, to even dream of finding let alone catching such a monster? No. Not a bit of it!

First, though, put out of mind the belief that we have reached a British ceiling with the near-47lb record pike, caught in 1992 in Llandegfedd Reservoir in Wales. For its captor, Roy Lewis, to have alighted on the biggest pike in Britain (or perhaps even the biggest pike in vast Llandegfedd for that matter, or indeed the largest fish of any species in any given water bar perhaps 'tame' individual large carp introduced into some fisheries) would mean he had succeeded against astronomical odds given the huge amount of freshwater environments in these islands, and the numbers of fish that must inhabit them. Even in the modern carp fisheries where extra-large well-fed stock fish, some approaching record weight, can be caught with relative certainty, it doesn't automatically follow that the largest of these would be the largest carp alive in the land.

But could there really ever be a British pike weighing more than 60lbs - a huge weight - bearing in mind that this remarkable predatory species does not lend itself to being tamed, cosseted and stuffed with food in the same fashion as almost-tame big carp put into some fisheries to attract the angler's dollar? Certainly there might well be such a fish if you take the evidence of a gigantic Loch Lomond pike skull examined by erudite British pike fisherman Fred Buller and engineer and 'specimen-hunter' extaordinaire the late Dick Walker, the one-time holder of the British carp record, both men thoroughly reliable sources as they say in the media business. The length of a pike's head, snout to gill cover, expands in exact proportion to the rest of its body as it grows, throughout its life, and from this ratio can be deduced the whole length of the Loch Lomond fish. Using a pretty reliable weight-for-length scale often employed by pike fishermen to calculate the weight of a catch, the two men concluded that the head found in the marshes where the Endrick joins the loch must have belonged to a pike of around an incredible 70lb. Further to that, scuba divers in many of Britain's large waters - lakes, reservoirs and the like - have reported seeing very large pike, sometimes to their alarm although so far as is known no diver has ever been attacked by one of these big fish. Does it follow from the divers' experiences that very large pike are generally found in large bodies of water rather than in small ones? In many instances it does, but there is more to the picture than most people would think.

Anglers will know that every water that contains pike has a 'monster' of legend: it is natural for these stories to emerge and become more embroidered at every telling: pike that gulp down whole ducks on a summer evening, geese even, or maybe a small dog sent to fetch a stick...a fish hooked by old Fred Smith which took all 200 yards of 20lb breaking strain line off his reel then just kept on swimming - ping! - to leave him broken-hearted. Pike of such cunning and ferocity that it is impossible to think of them, let alone fish for them, without a shiver of fear...

While much of the folklore can be dismissed, it does stand to reason that there will be a 'biggest' fish in every pike-holding water, a very much sought-after fish to be dreamed about by anglers with anticipation and tackled with as much determination as setting out for a record fish, even if in reality it is only an 18 or 20-pounder.

What may be said with some certainty is that the 'biggest' fish, be it the legendary feared inhabitant of the duck pond or, indeed, the biggest pike in Britain, is that the fish will be a female, since male pike rarely grow above 10lbs or live so long as the females, and if she is at optimum weight she will be nearing spawning. Also, if she is as big as she is ever going to get (there will of course be environmental and priobably genetic reasons for differences in size, water to water), she may well only have a few years left to live. Viewed in these terms, our quarry begins to become personalised, so much so that she demands a name. 'Bronwen' once suggested itself to the angler we are looking at on the windswept loch, in deference to the British record-holder coming from Wales, until one day a name popped into his mind that had strong connections with pike taxonomy and even ancient heraldry, not to mention a special connection in his own life - Lucie. And there she is in her prime, hovering in some vastness of water, big paddle fins moving gently, large, cold and inscrutible eyes scanning for prey. She sums up what pike anglers are all obsessed with, whether we're tucked in the rushes beside the lake of a stately home or bobbing on a windswept loch in the bitterness of winter: we are all looking for Lucie.

The lone fisherman out on the loch is an erudite man, at least in the ways of fish and fishing. He knows all the arguments for and against the likelihood of success, historical arguments as well as current, as he draws on one oar and lifts it dripping from the water then ships it as quietly as possible while the little cockleshell dinghy swings. But he's been moored fruitlessly on the spot for more hours than he cares to think about, all the time trying to keep his light craft nosing into the buffeting wind and a black, heaving swell streaked with racing wind-lanes of yellow foam, wondering if any of his theorising was ever worth more than a passing thought.

Chapter 2

Not for the first time have men been driven to face the apparently insurmountable, risk extreme discomfort or tackle seemingly impossible odds for love of a female. And while we all perhaps have our own 'Lucies' to pursue, is there anything that can shorten the odds and win the hand of the true Lucie, the one and only, the 50, 60, 70-pounder, the biggest pike in Britain? There is, and at the risk of over-simplification, this is how it works:

The waters that contain pike are many and varied, from streams and drainage ditches to rivers, ponds, lakes and canals of many different sizes, but together making an enormous area of water. The main and indeed the only factor in all this water which is likely to support a truly big pike is a ready and reliable supply of easily-acquired food. That means, in the main, the presence of other species of fish, since the predator pike is at the top of the food chain. Any given water can only support so much 'mass' of resident fish - that is, it could, say, produce X-number of medium-sized fish, a much smaller number of larger fish, or an altogether larger number of small and stunted ones, or a mixture of all three - but by and large, if they were all put together, the overall weight would be roughly the same. If we examine this food factor, taking water-types one by one, we can start to eliminate those less likely to produce really big pike simply because there is not enough food available. Ditches and streams, as well as smaller drainage ditches, can be ruled out immediately because they clearly won't keep a large-bodied fish supplied with enough food - let alone give it room to turn around! Ditto the smaller ponds.

Larger ponds, lakes, flooded gravel pits and so on offer a much better chance for fish to grow larger, say to 20-25lb or even 30lb, particularly if these waters contain large shoals of common prey species like bream, rudd and roach. There's another limiting factor that comes in here, however - competition. The older bigger pike get, the more pike mouths there are to feed from their own progeny and their progeny's progeny year on year - in exponential numbers. Thus these pike are in effect the architects of their own size limitations. An exception would be a pike that has come to be the sole member of its species present in the water - highly unlikely, because even new lakes that have started out with no pike at all acquire some after a time through factors like herons carrying the sticky eggs on their legs, or adventurous small pike (and they can be *very* adventurous) entering the water along flood-swollen streams or ditches. So generally, good pike can come from these medium-size waters, but not truly exceptional ones. For example, Cheddar Reservoir in Somerset, a relatively modest-sized reservoir which has a long-held reputation for producing pike to 30lb, never produces fish very much larger because of these limiting factors. These same limitations, resulting in a similar ceiling for the size of their pike, also apply in canals and the larger water channels like the Fenland drains.

Rivers introduce another dynamic: flow. The fish of moderate-sized still waters and canals do not have to use some of the food they lay down as fat to create energy to battle a current, while river pike do. Indeed, in times of flood, river pike can find themselves short of food as well as having to use up a lot of their weight to create energy; small wonder they seek out backwaters, weirpools and calmer out-of-the-current bays (where there are almost certainly shoals of many other fish species sheltering) to wait for the water to go down, and small wonder they sometimes find themselves stranded in water meadows that have been flooded lagoons, and left high and dry. In general, then, these more energetic pike will not grow very large. But there are rivers which break this rule and regularly produce very big pike - the Wye is one. What's happening here then? The answer is extra food, and lots of it, in the form of migratory fish in addition to resident stocks of coarse fish and trout.

Wye pike can not only feast on resident trout and coarse fish, but also on salmon and sea-trout running up the river to spawn, especially smaller grilse (salmon returning from the sea after just a year or so). They can also dine on weakened spent salmon (known as kelts) and dead ones (yes, pike scavenge too!) going back downriver. Then they can feed on the spring return to the sea of little salmon smolts and, as a bonus shared with some other salmon rivers, the upstream spawning run of herring-like shad from the sea in early summer. A smorgasbord indeed, and with the shad run in particular the bigger pike can virtually 'graze' without much effort and store away fat - very useful in a relatively fast-flowing river with high demands on energy.

Big fish from the Wye then - but there are two more situations which are even more favourable to pike, creating the haunts of monsters. First, the combination of large and generally placid lakes with rivers that deliver all the advantages that pike in the Wye enjoy. The massive system of rivers and lakes that contains huge Loch Lomond is a good example, and it has another significant additional source of food - shoals of resident herring-like deep water whitefish called powan (an ice-age relict and relative of the salmon) which in January move into the shallows to spawn. Easy living indeed.

Are we starting to narrow things down here in our hunt for Lucie? Seems like it. Think of other large, still waters where there are supplies of migratory fish in addition to resident feed species, and you come up with some of the major Scottish big pike fishing venues linked with river systems, including Loch Lomond and Loch Ken, not to mention Ireland's immense Lough Derg in the Shannon system: all are connected with pike monsters. Legend has it that 90lb pike have been caught in Ireland! We should not be all that surprised because Irish loughs also have their own version of Loch Lomond's shoalling powan: the pollan.

Remember, however, that Britain's current record pike came not from one of these locations, but from a reservoir. So what is special about Llandegfedd, and for that matter Chew and Grafham reservoirs in England where 30-pounders are regular and the records for the waters are continually edging up? What makes them able to produce these big fish even though they have no runs of migratory species or resident powan? Well, their success in growing these very big pike has little to do with their populations of resident coarse fish, though these are pretty good, and everything to do with being heavily stocked for trout fishing, particularly with rainbow trout. Thousands of tonnes of 'stockies' go into these waters every trout season, and apart from those relative few caught by fly fishermen most of them disappear without trace - in fact a scant few even actually manage to overwinter. Wonder where the others went...

You can't call any fish stupid, because they patently are masters of their own environment, but some (certainly not pike!) can be very unwary: often the trout-reservoir rainbows have been reared in large netting pens floating on the surface in open water where pike can inspect them without gaining access, which must be quite frustrating for the pike. Rainbows might well be instinctively wary of predatory fish, but if they are familiarised with pike on a daily basis without coming to any harm, they are not going to be terribly difficult to fall prey to one once they are released. Reservoir rainbows are often quite happy swimming round or even through your legs while you are fishing, perhaps waiting for someone to throw them a handful of food pellets. To pike, as well as to anglers, they seem to be saying: "I'm yours, take me."

So, big, big clues in the hunt for Lucie: she could well be lurking in a whitefish-rich Scottish or Irish loch which is connected with a game river, or in one of our larger reservoirs regularly stocked with trout. The wise gambler would still put his money on Scotland or Ireland, for the moment, while not ruling out the reservoirs entirely, since runs of salmon and other migratory fish in a lot of river systems, as well as resident whitefish like powan and pollan, have taken a knock in recent years. And so far as lochs go, it would certainly be a good idea to concentrate efforts at the points the rivers enter and leave, particularly spots where kelts and severely weakened or dead fish will waft to the bottom once the flow has stopped impelling them. That's where a substantial dead bait could at last earn you, finally, your meeting with Lucie.

It would be terrible, however, if such considerations disillusioned anyone who believes record pike could lie in waters other than those singled out just above. These are theories only, and monsters could indeed wait elsewhere. Odds on, though, it will be a place where the living is easy, and this is something to bear in mind if you want a good chance of becoming Lucie's successful suitor. Oh, and - like the lone figure on the loch - you'll need a high degree of perseverance.

Chapter 3

The fisherman has been in more comfortable conditions, that's a fact. The current is trying all the time to push him back broadside to the blow, where slops and spray come over the scant freeboard. Already there's more unwanted water in the bottom of the boat than he's happy about, and the cold and damp are starting to find their way into the core of remaining warmth. The light's going too, but he can still make out the orange blob of his fat balsa wood float, fifty yards off towards the dark gulf of the river's mouth, where he dropped a mackerel bait before drifting back to softly lower the old cast-iron bogey wheel from a granite quarry trolley that is now lying six or seven feet down. His grubby white fibreglass boat is bucking and tugging, tugging, tugging against this anchor's immovability, twanging the taut securing rope from time to time. Nearby hills vanished into drizzly grey long ago, let alone the more distant peaks, although the shoreline (where a few lights in the few waterside homes are starting to be lit) is still visible, as is some of the sweep of the glacial slope up out of the loch valley. "I'll stay for an hour more, maximum," he promises himself. It's exactly what he said more than an hour ago.

The flat slap of a breaching salmon comes from behind, to his left, and he turns his head to see the mark it has left; a good fish, maybe. Theorists say salmon are trying to dislodge sea lice digging under their scales when they jump, but this one has left the sea behind some days ago and cannot have any lice left, since they soon perish in fresh water. And anyway the fisherman prefers another version he once heard an old ghillie say, in soft lilt with bushy red eyebrows raised, "ay, he's just popped up for a look to see where he is." A recent spate has all but run off from the river, the fisherman knows, but some salmon are still running. But then it's not salmon he's after. He turns to peer back for his orange float, the tell-tale marker that will show if a fish has taken his bait. It isn't there...

***

Ten yards back and just a bit more than a fathom deep she can see the boat, the rope, the weight, and now and then a passing salmon or a sea-trout, urgent, mostly solitary but sometimes two or three smaller ones at once, skittish because of the unfamiliarity of their surroundings after a year at sea. One solitary fish has just jumped between her and the boat. For some time the scent of a dead fish, a fish smelling strongly of the sea, has been drifting back to her, but she won't move while the silhouette of the boat stays. She can wait, even though she knows too there are two or three other pike ahead, all far smaller than her. If they take the fish, so what? There will be other dead and dying fish from the river at the tail-end of the spate. She isn't desperately hungry, no more than normal, anyway.

***

The fisherman takes the winding arm off the spool of his reel so that there will be no resistance, careful not to scuff his boots or rattle anything in the boat that will send sound waves through the water to an acutely-sensitive fish. He watches the line beginning to move loop by loop by loop from the tip of his rod into the black swell. His hand tightens on the handle of his rod.

The movement stops abruptly, loops hanging slack, but still the fishermen does not stir, holding his breath. Has the fish let go of the bait? Or is it turning it around so that it can swallow it head-first as pike prefer, offering no impediment to sliding down the gullet? All he can do is wait in that tense and expectant suspense that all anglers know only too well. Encouragingly, the float still has not bobbed back up. Then, slowly at first, the line begins to inch away again, and his heart misses a beat as it starts to snake out faster.

"Time enough," he says to himself, and quickly snapping the reel winding arm back into place he sweeps his rod up and over his shoulder. The line whips out of the water and comes to a sudden halt, taut, with the wind whistling around it in an aolian whine of protest. There's a responding kick at the other end. He drops his rod to gain a yard or two of line on his reel and then gently puts the pressure back on again, trying to judge what he is up against. At least, with that kick, it's a fish, and not a tree stump or a mass of rotten weed.

It's not a long battle. In fact for three minutes or so the fish puts up no fight at all, as if it hasn't realised it has been hooked, and the fisherman manages to steadily get in quite a bit of line. But once the pike sees the boat, with the fisherman readying a huge landing net, it suddenly explodes into action, first driving deep then coming to the surface in a rush, nosing high into the air and thrashing with its tail so that it skitters over the surface, tail-walking and shaking its head to loose the hook's hold - impressive even with small pike but quite spectacular with an 15-pounder like this. Though he's geared up for a much bigger quarry, the fisherman still needs all his skill to bring it safely to the net, lift it aboard and gently tease-out the hook-holds in the perilously toothy mouth, taking a moment to admire the handsome gold and green striped fish in the dying light. Then he slides it gently back into the loch to swim free.

***

By the time the fisherman has broken down his tackle, stowed it and pulled

11

up the heavy iron anchor, he has only the distant light of a shore-side hotel amid a few other lamps in a scattering of homes to guide him safely towards his landfall.

***

After watching the episode impassively from her lie, moving only slightly aside to avoid the cloud of grey silt that drifted back to her when the weight was hauled up on its rope, the big fish is listening to the dying creak, creak of the departing fisherman's oars. Satisfied he is still moving away she widens her enormous light-gathering eyes and sets out on a patrol. Four or five times a day, more often than not, she makes this same circuit, a wide, slow curve almost up to the river's mouth where she can swing broadside to the current and drift gently and effortlessly back to her lie, scanning with all her senses for food as she goes. Tonight she strikes lucky almost as soon as she has made her turn at the river mouth, a grilse of about 6lb, a fish that has already been hit hard by another pike, perhaps, an otter, or more probably a cormorant trying to bite off more than it can chew in the way they do. Too late for death from the sky; the ospreys have all fled for the warmth of Africa. The grilse, a hen fish, is bravely trying to struggle on with a deep and whitening gash along one flank. It isn't anything of a chase, for the young salmon has little strength left. It isn't going to get better or make it to the upriver spawning beds and if the great pike knows any compassion, which it does not, despatching it is an act of mercy. Drifting back the rest of the way to her lie while she swallows her last meal of the day, the pike stops abreast of the shallow depression in the loch bed to swing her huge bulk about and settle down for the night, rest, digest.

Chapter 4

Mark Kendal still has to fight the wind and the boat is not helping him. It's sluggish as a sack of potatoes because of the weight of water it has shipped, but he cannot at this stage be bothered to bale out. He knows his steady, rhythmic oar strokes are shortening the distance he has to cover to the foreshore below the Glenside Rest. Soon the wind drops away under the protection of the steep valley side. The water quietens too now, waves no longer slapping the sides, and the going is easier, faster. Minutes later the black bulk of a stand of alders looms to the side of the white strip of sand and he makes for this. Judging when has the momentum just right, he ships his oars to let the dinghy's nose run aground with a crunch beside the low trees.

Moving quickly before she starts to slip back, he steps up to the nose, grabs the end of the bow painter and steps quite nimbly for a biggish man onto dry land. Hauling on the rope he pulls more of the boat ashore, then goes back on board to offload his tackle, placing it higher up the beach, and the oars, which for the moment he pushes under some of the low branches of the alder where no joy-riders can find them. As added security he takes the painter's end to the water's edge and some submerged branches where he makes it fast, then pushes the boat back out with his boot; the water in its bottom can stay there for the time being as a further disincentive to night trippers. It doesn't even matter much if she sinks completely in the night; it'll be easy enough to tip the water out in the morning. He shoulders his tackle box, picks up his rod and heads for the hotel car park and the campervan, his home from home.

Out of the blow on the loch his face has already started to glow warmly but it's when he's taken his outer waterproof layer off and stepped inside that he really feels the afterburn from wind and weather exposure. Sure enough the little mirror above the tiny sink shows a bright red face, and wind-tangled black-grey hair. It's not a big space inside the van, and he stows his tackle forward in the cab, then takes off his boots before taking a moment to towel his hair to a dryish state and going to the little galley in his socks to light a burner under the already-filled kettle. A heavy patter of rain from overhanging trees hits the roof, and there's a slight sway as a buffet of wind wobbles the van on her springs. At least he's out of all that now, thank God! He sits on his bed-cum-bench seat - currently in made-up bed mode - picks up a moblile phone lying on the tiny table he can barely get his knees under, and switches it on. When it finds a signal - not always a strong one in this hill-encircled spot - there's one voice message, from Jenny, his daughter.

"It's Mab, dad. I don't want you to worry, but she's had another fall. Bethlehem House has it all under control and she seems all right physically, but they want to find out what's making her keel over. Another mini-stroke, perhaps? Call me?"

He calls, anxious.

"It's me. How's your mum?"

"Hello...hang on a moment, I'm just putting Harry to bed...there! He was half asleep already. Okay now. Well, nothing more than I've told you really. She doesn't remember anything about it, of course. The doctor's seen her but seems very un-flapped and says he'll have to wait for test results. I expect he sees this sort of thing all the time, but it doesn't really help us, does it?"

Her voice does not betray any marked degree of strain, so there's a relief.

"I could come down if you think I should. I could get a fast train from Glasgow." Kendal, frowns. He stands to attend to the kettle with one hand, keeping the phone clapped to his ear.

"No, I don't think that's needed. Not right now, anyway. I don't think it's any worse than the other times."

"Sure?"

"Yes, for the time being anyway. It's all stable so don't worry, and I can let you know how things are going. How are you? And how's the fishing? Have you caught that big pike yet?"

He's relieved - it seems not so serious as it might have been. He's confident of his daughter's assessments.

"I've caught some pike."

"But not the right one, eh? No matter, there's always tomorrow. Unless she gets away."

Kendal grimaces. "There's an element of luck, you understand."

"I know. But are you coping all right up there on your own? The weather looks awful in Scotland every time I see the forecast. Biblical amounts of rain, gales...I mean, isn't it too ghastly to bother with? Tomorrow looks especially dreadful - dire in fact. And from then on it gets even more foul."

"Hey, I'm living in a pub car park, remember?" Kendal says wryly, pulling on his free ear and grinning. "There are worse places to be."

After he's asked after everyone else he finishes the call with a few pleasantries and a promise to charge his phone up at the hotel and take it with him tomorrow, keep it switched on in case there's any more news. Poor Mab, what a wretched existence, no matter how comfortable and well cared for she is in Bethlehem House. No way to end your days, that's a fact. And Kendal, now frowning again, remembers at the same time that Mab is a 'Lucie' too - so named because her parents were fans of Mabel Lucy Attwell - and she was

14

a Lucy who certainly did not get away. Not until all her present problems started happening, anyway, and then she got away good. Where the girl he loved had gone was another matter, into some other dimension perhaps, or more likely somewhere irretrievably deep within the unfathomable memory banks of her own head...and as he thinks about this the retired journalist feels a stab of worry about his own memory, or more precisely the growing unreliability of it. Surely he couldn't be going down the same road? God forbid!

***

It had started quite without warning, Mab's decline. He'd come home from work on press day - late as usual getting the paper away to the printers - and supper was ready. She brought two plates with pork chops for each of them from the warm oven, setting them in their laid-out places before bringing potatoes...a massive dish of potatoes, enough for at least six people, and six people with good appetites come to that.

"Hey," he had said, at this stage not realising anything was amiss, "Who else is coming?"

"What do you mean?"

"Isn't that rather a lot?"

She had looked at the dish, frowning, as if it was the first time she had noticed it.

"I suppose it is, now you come to mention it. Silly me. I expect I'll use them up somehow. Shepherd's pie perhaps."

She flashed one of her lovely smiles, and Kendal had thought no more of it until the next evening when a saucepan of milk for cocoa boiled over and burned on the hotplate to set the smoke alarm piping. Little instances of memory lapse started to become more noticeable after that, and it worried him so much that after a while he had suggested a visit to the doctor - not an easy proposal to make to someone when you can't fully explain the dark thoughts behind fear.

"All right, but it's just to reassure you," she had said in the end. "I'm quite sure I'm fine. Just a bit forgetful sometimes. We're all like that, aren't we? So do stop worrying."

This condescension for a check-up on her part had brought him a little relief, but the doctor's confidential prognosis did not, nor did the follow-up session with specialist ever-smiling Chinese Dr Ran: diagnosis? Mild but all the same progressive dementia, a little early but not uncommon. Treatment? Drugs, efficacy uncertain. Prognosis grimmer: eventual decline inevitable. And a couple of years later, there had been a mini-stroke and he'd found to his shame that he'd been unable to lift his own wife to her feet. The need for specialist care had become more and more pressing. And now, at this stage down the line, all he and their daughter really saw of the old Mab, from time to time, was a flash of her smile, like the Cheshire cat's smile, although not at all comical. Whenever it happened it reawakened countless happy memories, and at the same time it ripped his heart to shreds.

***

There is a good inch of standing water over the entire surface of the Glenside Rest car park as Kendal makes his way to the hotel under a hissing umbrella after finishing a cold meat pie with his mug of tea. Under a wildly-swinging sign he pushes open the door and steps into the heavy-carpeted warmth of the foyer, folds and drops his dripping brolly in the waiting stand and heads for the bar. The comfortable surroundings lift his spirits a little but he still feels an underlying air of gloom which he cannot shake: a drink or two will probably help.

"And as soon as Jimmy clears all the shilly-shanky spiders out of the hoose they're back again, only more, more, more every time."

He's not the only one with a grump on going by the tone of the conversation he walks into: wheelchair-bound Alastair Sutherland is ranting at the barman, John, a red-haired young man who is nodding without perhaps listening at all attentively and carrying out every barman's Sisyphian task of polishing glasses. There's a click of pool balls in the adjoining side bar: probably Jimmy, Alastair's minder and housekeeper. Closer, he sees it is indeed Jimmy, playing a local lad who Kendal cannot yet recognise because he can only see his back. The five, including Kendal, are the only inhabitants of this part of the hotel - perhaps the entire hotel.

"It's another one of God's little jokes, like sending us out fishing on a day like this, wouldn't you say, fisherman?"

Kendal returns the recognition with a gesture but straggle-haired Alastair is in full heavily accented flow (characteristically so after a few drinks) sitting with a tartan rug over his knees, his chariot slewed sideways to the long mahogany bar, his somewhat wild eyes with their jutting tufts of orange eyebrows just about level with it.

"Now these little beggars are so, so grateful for a few tiny midges, a wee piece of protein. Why should they be doomed to live like this when they could go in the larder and nibble at my cheese instead, like the mice? Come to that, why don't they eat crap, like most wee creatures do? Then they wouldn't have to spend all day hanging upside down on the ceiling. There's plenty of crap around in this life, isn't there, fisherman?"

The barman looks around as if he's worried sensitive souls might overhear the Scotsman's crudities, though he knows there's no-one to be offended

16

within a mile. He holds up a pint glass and gets a nod from Kendal, a silent transaction - the usual. Kendal shrugs. It can't be denied, there's a lot of crap about. He knows Alastair's particular ration of 'crap' is a full-blown stroke he's been trying to fight his way back from for the last two years. At least Alastair, an ex-soldier and like Kendal in his late 60s, has got all his marbles, and more than that he has a chance of full recovery.

"The only blessing we have is a drink or two," Alastair goes on. "God says, 'Ah, let's tease the poor wee things. Here, man, stick a bit of grain in some water, drain it off after a bit, then drink it. There, you like that don't you? Now, leave it a bit longer, distil the essence from it, and drink that too as a chaser - even better, eh? And, ho ho, wait and see what it does to your poor wee head in the morning'. Did y'catch anything today?"

"Only one. About 15 pounds. Late on, too." Kendal pays for his drink, sips for a taste and then takes a deeper draught.

"So our baby's still out there, eh? She'll be so big now she'll swallow you along with that little boat of yours."

"She might enjoy the boat. I think she'd find me a bit on the tough side."

Even though it's an oft-repeated story he's heard from Alastair since he set up home in the car park for the past two autumns, Kendal feels a shiver of excitement. A pike as long as the boat, Alastair had said on one occasion, and "I wouldna believe it if I hadn't seen it wi' my own eyes." Even if it were half the length of his boat, making it a six-footer, it would still be a truly remarkable pike, the Mona weight-for-length scale used by fishermen to assess their catch stopping at five feet and representing a probable weight of more than 67lb.

"And even if she did gobble me up you'd never know about it, would you?" Kendal goes on, glad of the conversation even at this fairly banal level - its has been a long and lonely day in the boat, and he's not an anti-social man, except perhaps when fishing. "There'd only be my van in the yard left and for all you know I could be somewhere else for the day, a week, more. And let's face it, who would miss me?"

Alastair looks away and Kendal has the feeling the sentiment has not gone down too well. Perhaps it's too close to the mark, a self-fulfilling prophesy? To make amends he buys Alastair and the barman a drink, and then the pool players from the games room appear while John goes over to the fire to make it up with some wiry unsplit oak logs, green with dried lichen, which flare to a spitting blaze. Jimmy's pool opponent, Kendal now sees, is a lad called Rory - second name unknown, or rather unremembered - who is visiting from the other side of the loch. As the two join them Alastair clutches at the young man's sleeve and pulls him down.

"You tell this man here about the big pike that comes up to the river bridge every now and then. You tell him why you and the other village boys never go in the water there."

His captive does not back him up.

"I've never seen anything," the dark lad says, and Alastair frowns, lets go of his sleeve.

"But it doesn't alter the fact the boys won't go in the water there, does it?"

Rory shakes his head.

"No - I guess so," he says reluctantly, then to Kendal: "No, they don't. But I don't know why."

"There! You see!" says Alastair, triumphant.

Sensing the lad's embarrassment Kendal moves to change the subject, even though it's of great interest to him.

"Has anyone heard what the weather might be like tomorrow?"

"Wet!" they chorus in unison.

***

The lad is the first to leave the hotel - it's a ten mile trip to his village round the head of the loch, across the very bridge they've been talking about. The barman has pointedly cashed up his till, the evening's takings so far not at all making up the cost of his labour and not likely to either, no matter how long he stays open.

"Will you be wanting more bait?"

Everyone has taken the hint and Kendal will be last out of the door.

"One packet, I guess. Mackerel please. How many does that leave John?"

"Three more, I'd say, though I'm not sure. I'll tell you in a minute." He disappears.

Kendal has a weekly order with the fish man who supplies the hotel: ten large fresh herring, ten large fresh mackerel; each time they arrive he divides them into packs of five of each, and the hotel kindly stores them for him in a corner of its copious freezer. His gas-powered campervan fridge has barely enough room for a couple of rashers of bacon. He's offered to pay for this convenience but this has been waved away as unnecessary. So far, with the fishing being so slow, he has built up a surplus that will overlap with tomorrow, Friday's delivery. Too late, alas, to phone the supplier and stop the delivery. Oh well, at least all but one of the baits he's used so far has caught fish, the best a 23-pounder.

The barman returns and a solid lump of frozen fish thuds onto the bar.

"Two herring, one mackerel left."

With Jimmy wheeling Alastair off across the swimming car park into a mist of rain, covered in a vast old yellow oilskin bicycle cape and an outsize tam-o-shanter, Kendal crosses to his van. To prevent the inside stinking of fish the bait goes with those left over from today under an upturned bucket by the door with a large rock on it to stop the foxes geting a free meal. He has one more task - in a bedside notebook (the paper limp from condensation) he quickly scribbles a reminder to himself: "Bait; food; switch off gas and light; phone Jenny; charge phone tomorrow night. Don't forget camera". He smiles wryly, wondering when it was that he never had the need to supplement his memory in this way. Afterwards, he's quickly out of his clothes and in his sleeping bag and - thanks to the alcohol just as much as a strenuous day - just as quickly asleep.

***

Our big fish, however, does not sleep, at least not in the sense that we do, out of it, unconscious. Even at her age and great size she keeps some of her senses on guard, wary. She has learned to do so ever since she hatched.

A gloriously wicked piece of work, the Pike, the Luce, the *Water Wolf*: a long, lean killing machine, the ultimate hunter-killer, the unrivalled overlord of its environment, our largest native freshwater fish and a universally feared prowler and assassin of shadowy underwater canyons. It's a fish that earns the same awe expressed in the last line of William Blake's poem 'Tiger' when, after aghast appreciation of the big cat's 'fearful symmetry' he asks - "did God, who made the lamb, make *thee*?"

Look into those large, cold and pitiless eyes and try to hold back a shiver. Look at the shape and size of the fish: is there any doubt about the purpose of its design? What smaller fish's heart would not skip a beat as such a monster's menacing outline checks, then turns towards them? Only two options remain open to the prospective prey: flee, if you think you have a big enough start and the speed to make this practical, or freeze, come to a complete standstill and rely on camouflage, the invisibility-cloak trick that all fish can pull off to some extent.

Alas, that's not much use once the pike has tuned its unbelievably acute senses into your presence and has all its systems purring along with a turbo-power drive rippling under its skin, preparing to strike. All too soon, with a lightning surge, the monster is upon you. Too late to flee now. The last many a fish sees before oblivion is the onrush of those huge and terrible jaws opening, engulfing, clamping shut. And what jaws! A thousand needle-sharp teeth snap down to mesh with the fangs below, piercing scales, flesh. Resistance is futile, and the game is quickly over - a gulp usually turns the dinner around so that it can slide down the gullet head-first, the scene returns to calm, and the pike hovers immobile, placid, its gill covers softly opening and closing, an expression on its face that it would be hard not to call a grin (to the great 19th century pike angler Alfred G. Jardine, inventor of the livebaiter's snap-tackle, "a ghastly grin") while a few silvery scales waft gently towards the bottom. Assassin, *moi*?

In recent years there has been a tendency for anglers to kiss on the lips (each to his own!) large fish they have captured, an event often photographed for a keepsake to look at once the fish has been returned to the water. It's a good bet that few would want to bestow this dubious act of worship upon a pike's ugly, some would say cruel snout, let alone get anywhere near those lacerating teeth. And yet, overall, hardly anyone can deny that the pike is an object of terrible beauty, fully worthy of appreciation even if falling short of deserving a shower of kisses. And it's an extremely popular and universally well-known species, not just with fishermen - there must be few people who cannot describe a pike with some degree of accuracy, in contrast to which many who do not go fishing would be hard pressed to tell you the differences between, say, other common species such as roach and rudd, or chub and dace.

To be able to land a pike or haul one into a boat, especially a big pike (big or small it will fight every inch of the way), is a memorable experience and a real privilege. Small wonder fishermen want to study and admire their catch, albeit briefly, before returning it to the water. Small wonder also that they turn into pike-hunting fanatics like Kendal. Apart from that large, extended head and fearsome mouth, the main thing you notice is that this is a very long fish - torpedo shapes travel more easily through the water than squat, dumpy ones - and that it has three of its fins, large fins at that, clustered at the extreme end of its body. Together they form the motor for the final killer thrust, although these powerful paddles can also work more gently in unison with the fish's other fins for slow movement or cruising. It's a solid fish, too, broad of back, slab-flanked, most of it pure, hard muscle. And out of its element, the fish's coloration seems rakish, bold and even vivid - something it shares with close relatives in North America, such as the mighty look-alike Muskellunge of the Great lakes and the smaller and more widely distributed (but no less fierce) Pickerel. The overall base colour of the pike's mail-coat of copious but relatively small neat scales is a delicate green on those big flanks, shading upwards to a darker sage to olive back and beneath to a gold to cream belly. This is liberally blotched and barred with patterns of radiant gold. But however eye catching this may look in the open air - and frankly beautiful in a dreadful sense - once the fish is back underwater, lying in wait against a background of weeds and reed stems and bathed by the shifting patterns of light and shade coming through the rippled surface, despite all its very distinctive features our pike seems to fade away, to melt into its surroundings, to vanish.

Luckily for fishermen, a hungry pike is not terribly choosy - or all that cautious - about its food sources. Occasionally it may become fixated on a particularly plentiful and tasty supply provided by nature, such as a spawning run of shad or over-abundant shoals of bream or rudd, but otherwise "anything that moves" in the watery environment is fair game, provided it is not enormously large, including small to medium-sized water birds, mammals like the water vole and amphibians besides fish (however, little credance can be given to reported attacks on humans, or even dogs for that matter, unless the dog in question is fairly small). That said, hungry pike have been known to take on prey very close to their own size. And to "anything that moves" can be added "anything dead", particularly dead fish, for the pike is also a scavenger, thereby performing the vital role of garbage-collector/hygienist in the watery world. A herring or a sprat from the fishmonger, even a long-unfrozen and whiffy one, can make a very attractive bait. And there's even more than that on the menu when you take into account a flaw for which the pike ought perhaps to show an inkling of remorse (a personality disorder if you like) - it shows no guilt about eating its own kind. It is an unrepentant cannibal.

Small wonder most pike lead a mainly solitary existence and are extremely wary of one another, this from an early age too for pike of only a few inches can attack their own kind. As an occasional exception to this rule, for a limited time in spring male pike sometimes gather in quite large numbers to court a spawning female (often very, very much larger than themselves) but even in this highlight of their social calendar caution is a keynote and squabbles and out-and-out fights between suitors are far from uncommon.

While we can often only dream about what is going on beneath the reflective surface of our lakes, ponds, canals, rivers and streams, there are tell-tale signs which point to a hunting pike: sudden huge swirls in places one would not expect to find a big fish, for example, or a mysterious violent rattling of dried reed stems on a still winter day. Mother water-birds fussing around a string of small fluffy chicks become highly agitated, and justifiably so, when a pike is about, and occasionally you'll see the most obvious give-away of all when a shoal of small fish suddenly bursts from the surface in terror, scattering like raindrops in all directions.

These are sights that stir the heart of a pike angler, fuelling an overwhelming and lasting addiction. Just like a powerful drug, the attraction is deep and often unshakable. It will draw adherents out on the bitterest of winter days, in snow or lashing rain as well as in the balmy days of summer, and it can make them stay up all night watching a line for the slightest movement, hoping every next minute will bring the reward of a thrilling encounter. Most would be happy with a decent sized fish from, say, eight or nine pounds upwards (pike in the 5-8lb range are usually called Jack, or Jack-pike), but some are spurred on by the more ambitious aim to catch a fish of 20lb or more - rightly or wrongly a 'threshold' weight above which pike are deemed to be large, and at weights thereafter progressively more desirable with every additional ounce. The British ultimate, of course, is the capture of a fish that challenges Roy Lewis's current British rod-caught record pike of 46lb 13oz. It is not actually *totally* unchallenged - a 1945 capture of a 47lb fish by Tommy Morgan in Loch Lomond occupies the 'Scotland's best' slot even if unrecognised by the British Record (Rod-Caught) Fish Committee. Nor does either record represent a ceiling in pike weights, which some believe could go as high as 90lb (a verified rod caught fish of 50lb-plus has been recorded in Germany, where a 60lb-plus - not rod-caught - fish can also probably be regarded as genuine. Mighty big fish!). And as we've seen, even larger fish have been claimed...

Not everyone is motivated to catch pike just for the thrill of it or even to be able to boast about a big one, for it is also a large edible fish (if on the bony side) quite welcome on the table, forming a big part of the local cuisine particularly in inland places where historically there has been little chance of obtaining fresh sea fish.

Old toothy, however, is not welcomed or even liked by everyone. Fishery owners whose waters are full of expensive stock fish believe they have good reason to hate it, as do river-keepers trying to maintain good levels of trout, salmon and sea-trout in their waters. In some situations steps are taken to eradicate them - not necessarily justified, say conservationists, since a reasonable level of predation leads to the overall higher weight of individual fish, and the useful activity of scavenging dead fish can keep fish diseases in check. Great care is also being taken to stop pike spreading to waters throughout the world where they could readily damage delicate eco-systems: the introduction of carp to Australia's Murray-Darling River system, for example, has been little short of a disaster, especially for the once-common mighty Murray cod. Heaven only knows what damage pike could cause in some sensitive environments.

Within its native range, which broadly speaking is much of the northern half of the Northern Hemisphere (in North America it is mainly known as the Northern Pike, not to be confused with the closely related muskellunge or the pickerel), Esox lucius is only discouraged in a few locations and has little to challenge its supremacy as top predator, thriving in all situations where it is not persecuted or over-fished. Long may it continue to stalk with impunity, if only to remind us that the environment it inhabits and part-shares with our own world can be an alien, untameable and savage place where life is cheap and where being big and merciless is a great advantage for survival.

Much archive matter and literature has been built up regarding this fearsome predator, as well as (according to Frank Buckland in The Natural History of British Fishes, 1880) "more lies than about any other fish in the world". Not surprisingly for such a striking fish, it even has a place in heraldry as the "Lucie", taking pride of place alongside unicorns and lions rampant and couchant. Fitting, for such a remarkable animal.

Chapter 5

It's nearly half past eight when Kendal rouses himself, switches on his little digital radio for the news and a weather forecast and starts to dress. He's felt no pressure to rise very early. In this latitude and at this time of year the sun's been up for barely half an hour, and just before 6pm it will dive below the horizon again - a far, far cry from the long days of a Scottish summer. The bright and apparently clear sky of the morning does not fool him one bit, and he opens the door, sniffs the freshness of it all, steps down from the van, and takes himself to the middle of the car park to get a clear view all round. The south west gale that has battered the van most of the night has blown itself out, but scattered twigs and yellow leaves thick on the ground bear testament to its ferocity. Now there is a lull, no discernible direction to the movement of air, a dithery, uneasy sort of peace. He looks to the north west, where the forecast says the next bout of weather will come from. There's nothing obvious in sight but beyond the tops of the glen ridges he can see quite clearly all the way to two high middle-distance peaks and a good way beyond, bringing to mind the local saying often trotted out for visitors: If you can't see the mountains, it's raining; if you can see the mountains, it's going to rain. Another day at the office then! But to his right now, the loch looks flat calm, and the boat is still afloat by the alders. So far so good.

Rather than using up the scant amount of drinking water carried in his campervan tank Kendal has been using a little mountain burn that runs down the edge of the car park for his ablutions but today he can see it is brown and running high and fast. After going back to the van for his toothbrush he cleans his teeth and splashes his face with bracingly chilly water in the washbasin in the hotel's beer-garden loos, mercifully never locked, a facility sanctioned by Angus McReady, the hotel's owner. Mr and Mrs McReady, taking advantage of the fall-off in trade that always comes at this time of the year, are away, taking a month's break in the Canaries ("They all do it at this time of the year, all the way across the land," John the barman has recently observed with some relish. "They all go off to sleep with each other's wives and husbands and once they've got that out of their system they're just about ready for Christmas and Hogmanay."). Kendal is more than grateful for the hospitality shown by the McReadys and indeed everyone in this little community, and he's certainly not prepared to pass judgment on the morals of Scottish hoteliers even if they're as lascivious as they have been painted. He boils a kettle of water, makes tea and a small flask of black coffee, eats half a chocolate swiss roll for his breakfast and throws two meat pies and an apple into a carrier bag with the flask; that's him set for the day.

After first making himself as waterproof as possible against the worst this day might chuck at him, Kendal hauls his tackle, bait and food to the shore. He finds the painter end and hauls the boat as far up the beach as he can get her. She has shipped quite a bit more water, but by lifting one side and rocking gently he starts slopping it out. Good job he hadn't fitted heavy bottom boards as had been advised, he observes. With a final effort he can roll the boat on its side almost to the vertical, which loses all the water left - well, all that matters. That done he stows his tackle, retrieves the oars, pushes the boat out until the water is almost up to his boot-tops and the stern is just afloat, and jumps aboard. Hauling up the bogey-wheel , he first poles away from the shore with an oar and then sits to row when he's over deep enough water. Without the drag of extra water in the bottom of the boat, and the light, flat going, progress is swift, the creak of the oars almost musical - there's even a wake across the calm surface now. Coots call, somewhere a heron. A flight of three swans is heading majestically in the direction he is going, and even with the boat noises he can hear the steady whoosh, whoosh of their wings. Even though it's a late start by his standards, the air is still morning-fresh and Kendal has that rush of anticipation that all anglers know well: What will today bring? He pauses and ships oars to put up one rod, three pieces, an 11-footer with a bit of backbone. Rummaging in his tackle bag he finds a reel to suit, threads up his line and finds and ties on - for the moment - a plug, green and red floating wooden lure with a scooped piece of metal at the nose which will make it dive when it is drawn through the water. In this way he can cover the vastness of the middle of the loch on the way to his destination: there might be a pike or two around to hit it, even though the lure might not dive to more than six feet or so. He flicks the lure astern and lets off around 40 yards of line before clicking the reel's winding arm on, and props the rod over the crook between the transom and gunwale. He settles back to pick up his oars, lines himself up on course and starts to pull eagerly for the river end of the loch, spirits high.

***

Lucie can hear him coming again. In fact her senses are so acute she's been aware of his distant presence on the water ever since he launched the dinghy. His approach is starting to become familiar, shifting to an area of her mind where she's no longer quite so suspicious about his activities.

Unlike Kendal, she's been up and about long before daybreak, spurred to move by a pressing hunger and a hormonal shift that is always likely to strike her at this time of year, and breakfasted on another grilse that was wavering, unsure of its way. Now, still hungry, she is about to set forth on another patrol, and no longer sees any reason why she should be delayed by the inexplicable activities of man.

The fish that spawned her had also been a large one, and was able to pass this genetic marker down to her offspring. Some 25 springs ago, losing her appetite to feed and driven by an unbidden urge, she had arrived by the shallows at the river mouth and started to push herself deeper and deeper into the weedy bay to spawn. As she did so, moving on through water growing shallower and more weedy all the time, she began to encounter other pike. They were mainly males, many of them small enough to have been eaten without a blink, swallowed whole had she so wished; normally they would have avoided her but now, as she passed, they began to follow her closely, as if drawn after her by invisible threads. All it would take to fill her stomach would be one quick turn and a snatch! This was a time of year, however, when many of the otherwise important rules of survival like keeping out of each others' way had to be ignored. She very soon had a train of 15, perhaps more male pike fanning out behind her in an ill-tempered,snappy and quarrelsome pack.

***

For Lucie today, spring is still some way ahead. However, her body is preparing for it. Long sacs are starting to swell in her commodious abdominal cavity, and at the appointed time they will be packed with hard, long roes each containing thousands upon thousands of fully-developed eggs, every one of them primed to carry her species forward. It has been thus since long before men appeared on the earth, and indeed her very successful species may yet survive humankind. As with the matriarch which spawned her many years ago, October has brought with it a growing hunger; she not only has to raise her body weight to help her survive winter, which can be bitter in these parts, but she also has to divert much of the protein she eats into eggs. Like the fisherman, Lucie is on a mission; and also like him she does not fully understand why this is so, or what is motivating her. But eat she must at this time of year and - if possible - do so regularly and copiously.

To imagine that Lucie's world as she sets out on a patrol is anything like our own - indeed to imagine we can imagine what it is like - would be folly. Even if we could be comfortable underwater, which we never truly are, we lack her acute senses, as indeed we lack all the senses of any fish. For example, we cannot detect (at least not consciously) minute changes in pressure in the medium we live in - the air - let alone in water. In fish, the sensors provided for this can not only detect the movement of other creatures in the water around them, often for some distance, but also register the footfall of anything walking along the bank, perhaps even being able to distinguish between four-footed and two-footed animals. And some fish - pike perhaps among them, though this hasn't been ascertained for sure - can detect the minute electrical discharges given off by other living organisms. Added to that, Lucie's hearing is acute (sound travels very easily in water), her senses of smell and taste can pick up traces of possible foodstuff - especially blood from a wounded fish - at incredibly enormous dilutions and over great distances. And her eyes...her eyes are huge.

***

Almost imperceptibly, no more visible than her own vague shadow on the loch bed, Lucie begins to drift sideways off her lie to her right. The thick, rich dark black blood that surges along the big artery just below her backbone, carrying oxygen from her lacy armour-plated gills to ever-smaller veins and through capilliaries to tight, hard-packed layers of muscle, hardly moves any faster. Her body is practically the same density as the water around her, which means she can hear and feel her life-force sloop, sloop, slooping along her body, feeding not only the motor but all her other controls - fins to adjust speed, attitude and direction, fins to accelerate and drive with concentrated force and - when necessary - fins that can bring her to an abrupt halt.

At this time of year, with grilse as well as more mature and often very big salmon running, it would be profitable to stay in her lie and pick off the odd straggler, were it not for the fact that the bright morning has interrupted the salmon run and they are holding back in deeper water. If it clouds over, they may start to move again but today she is far too restless to wait for the weather to change, even if she can sense a tiny drop in water-pressure. The atmospheric jet stream, tugging low-pressure systems to its left and high pressure to the right, is shifting. More rain will be on its way, this time from another direction.

For some way from her lie to the loch shore, the depth stays at 6ft or so and there is little in the way of features on the bed, mainly because of layer after layer of silt brought down over the years by the river: it settles out here, where the flow lessens, a smooth grey carpet. Because of impurities in the water Lucie is unable to see clearly a very long way in any direction, although unlike many fish her eye sockets are set on the top of her head rather than the sides: she can therefore look forward and synchronise both fields of vision (though each eye can move independently of the other), vital for striking accurately at her prey and also for conning ahead. Although she cannot see in colour - she has mainly highly sensitive black-and-white light detecting rod receptors in her eyes - her vision is so acute that most colours are distinguishable even in shades of grey, making the worth of 'colour vision' as we know it arguable.

Some river-wash from last night's rain is still staining the water so there's an impenetrable brown-grey mist after 20 yards all round. Upwards, she has an elongated oval view of the surface for a slightly smaller distance, an unruffled mirror at the moment with a bright sky beyond. Towards the river mouth, sitting and fussily preening in this upside-down world, legs dangling, is a flock of black-headed gulls, and a moorhen is skirting them to reach the distant shore. Birds like this have been prey in the past, with the pike shooting up from the depths to catch them unawares, but Lucie has ceased to bother with them. Too insubstantial, mostly feathers - now she is mostly concerned with fish, high protein sustenance and easy to digest. Ignoring the birds she moves on with a plan and with her senses set at full alert. She's mainly concerned with a periphery of about 50 yards around her, and although she has already identified the approaching fisherman she also knows a herd of Angus cattle is moving very slowly across the bankside meadow she's headed for, tearing tufts off the rough grass with leathery tongues and, one by one, sitting down heavily to chew the cud and await the rain, stomachs rumbling. On the other bank, the school bus-cum-post delivery has already passed, followed by a couple of cars, and now a delivery van has pulled up at the hotel, its engine left running. Behind her and beyond the limits of her senses, she knows, the loch is immensely long, widening as it goes to more than a mile before narrowing again to the outlet 24 miles away. It goes much deeper too, plunging into a chasm gouged out by an ice-age glacier, and there are islands, mounds of boulders, grit and pebbles left where the melting ice dumped them. The high tops of the ridges along the valley cradling the loch are a testament to just how huge and how powerful the glacier must have been, how much compressed steely blue ice was packed within it. A village, waking up with a medley of noises, lies behind her on the same bank as the cows and almost opposite the hotel.

Still slipping quietly sideways through largely weed-free water without moving forward, she has seen very few fish so far - a few small perch chasing one another mid-water, ruffe, and gudgeon rooting in the silt. As with the birds, the effort of chasing them isn't worth the outcome. They seem to know this, moving aside a little way to let her pass but not bothering to flee. Flutters of their movements ripple along the pressure sensors running along her flanks from head to tail as she passes, while other detectors in little pits on her underslung jaw pick up minute prickly electrical pulses. However, she has bigger prey in mind, and as the water begins to get shallower she gears all these senses up a few notches, along with her caution: hunting from here on demands stealth.

There are curtains of weed now, yellow-brown, dying back and fragile, and with every foot the pike has to rise, her view of the encircling surface grows correspondingly smaller: she focuses ahead and when a forest of still-green bankside lilies and reed stems marks the water's edge, she ends her sideways drift and starts to edge forward.

***

You can hardly see them moving, the fisherman remembers from his boyhood as he reaches his objective and gently, ever so gently, lets down his bogey-wheel anchor. But moving they are...

***

"Remember that bloody big pike we caught?"

It's 1958, and the words are being spoken to Prof Alan Quatermass to stop his mind being taken over by some extremely unpleasant Martians, which look rather like hobgoblins, in a science fiction serial on TV: "Quatermass and the Pit".

It isn't the only motivation that sees the 12-year-old Mark Kendal, Pete Jones and Dave Brown looking down on the partly-frozen surface of Brightwell Lake on a bitterly cold late November day, but it is fresh in all their minds and a phrase timely and aptly reproduced as the three watch the long shadowy shape moving through the patches of brown weed towards their waiting baits. They're on a high bank between bare trees which gives them a good view of the shallows. George Sanders, the school groundkeeper, had given them leave to raid the grass mowings heap for brandling worms, and they'd then gathered at the Brightwell estate office to pay over their pennies for permits, goggling at the 20lb stuffed pike in a glass case on the wall. With the worms, they'd caught silver bream at the dam end, and these are the baits now dangling from big cork bungs in one of the largest clearings in the weed.

***

Dave is rugged up in a heavy coat and scarves and a thick balaclava and looks a bit like a black snowman, but Pete and Mark, more lightly dressed, have tucked their bare hands under their armpits to try to warm them. Clouds of exhaled steamy breath surround all three.

"Is it moving?" Pete asks looking at the shape that has appeared from nowhere.

"I don't know. I think so," says Mark.

"Throw a rock at 'un," Dave suggests thickly from his dense mound of insulation.

Mark will do no such thing, for the pike is actually clear of the weed and closing in on his bait. A sudden rush and he has it in his jaws with Mark racing down the slope to strike and connect with the fish and the other boys tearing after him, helter skelter.

It isn't very big of course, and the fight to bring it in isn't a battle royal, but it's lovely to have it, unhook it, hold it for a moment and then release it. Only

29

when it has gone does it get bigger!

It's not his first encounter with a pike, but it is the first of many he will go on to catch. In the very first encounter he was at another, smaller lake fishing for roach and crucian carp, and he was just pulling in a very small silver roach that had taken a bait intended for better fish when there was a sudden swirl behind it and, right before his eyes, a huge mouth opened, a great onrushing gulf bristling with teeth. He'd been so shocked he had to step back, let the line go slack. And instead of engulfing the tiny fish the pike stopped dead, puzzled, glaring at him with huge, angry primeaval eyes before sliding back into the depths from which it had so suddenly appeared. He'd had to sit down, shaking. It had seemed like a challenge - a challenge to which he would never stop responding.

***

It may seem an odd notion to us, but some historical works on fishing and natural history hint at a not-so distant time when Britain had no pike at all in any of her waters. This is a difficult concept to contemplate, let alone prove, particularly when the species *Esox lucius* has a wide distribution in northern latitudes, North America as well as Eurasia. Fossils of the fish date from 62 million years ago (Canada) and it's believed Eurasian pike colonised North America ahead of the Ice Age, then got wiped out by glaciation and recolonised back from N America when the Bering Strait was a land bridge. However, it is likely England had low stocks after the Ice Age (first arriving when the Channel did not exist and when the Thames was a tributary of the Rhine) and recolonisation took some time. Fossil pike remains of considerable age have been found in East Anglia as have preserved bones from pre-Roman times - none of which prove conclusively that pike have had a continuous existence here since then. Most of Scotland, Ireland and Wales, it seems, were actually pike-free as recently as the Middle Ages (monks took pike, a valuable food fish, to Ireland in the 14th or 15th century) but this adventurous hunter has fully established itself in all these areas. In Europe, today, it is gradually spreading southwards into fresh territory, notably Spain.

The great nineteenth century fishing writer Frank Buckland (*The Natural History of British Fishes*, 1880) helpfully gives several of the names this fish goes by, including, in England, Luce, Pickerel (or Pickeral) and for small fish Jack, in Scotland, Gedd (from Norse), and in Wales, Penhwyad. The French call it Le Brochet, the Germans Der Hecht, also Wasserwolf. Buckland concludes: "The best name of all the above applied to the Pike is Waterwolf."

Writing earlier, and perhaps a little more clinically than Buckland, William Yarrell in *A History of British Fishes* (1836) details the numbers of rays in each fin of the fish: dorsal, 19; pectoral, 14; ventral, 10; anal, 17; caudal (tail) 19.

Yarrell's ray-counts, which he painstakingly notes for all British fish species, are partly intended as identification guides, which with a fish so distinctively shaped as the pike is largely academic compared with, say, distinguishing between a roach and a rudd.

Yarrell's observations on the life cycle of pike concur for the most part with modern data (some of it based, indeed, on his findings) except that he appears to have swallowed the following spurious tale about the fish's longevity: "Pliny (Roman Pliny the Elder, Naturalis Historia, 77-79) considered the pike as the longest lived, and likely to attain the largest size, of any freshwater fish. Pennant (Thomas, Welsh naturalist 1726-1798) refers to one that was ninety years old; but Gesner (Conrad, Swiss physician and naturalist, 1516-1565) relates that, in the year 1497, a pike was taken at Hailbrun in Saubia (today the South Baden-Wurttemberg region, Germany) with a brazen ring attached to it, on which were these words in Greek characters: - '*I am the fish which was first of all put into this lake by the hands of the Governor of the Universe, Frederick the Second, the fifth of October, 1230.*' This fish was therefore 267 years old, and was said to have weighed three hundred and fifty pounds. The skeleton, nineteen feet in length, was long preserved at Manheim as a great curiosity in natural history."

"Harrumph!" you can almost hear Frank Buckland saying some 40 years later as he writes in *The Natural History of British Fishes*, "From the days of Gesner downwards, more lies - to put it in very plain language - have been told about the pike than any other fish in the world; and the greater the improbability of the story, the more particularly it is to be quoted. Among these stories there can be no greater fabrication than that of the pike that is recorded to have lived 260-odd years. An account of this precious fish can be found in almost every angling book published. We are now in 1880, and supposing the fish to have been caught in this year, it follows he must have been put into the lake in 1630, the sixth year of the reign of Charles 1."

He adds the tetchy aside: "This story might have done very well years ago, but it will *not* do now."

Which is not to say pike are not long-lived: analysis of growth data in otoliths (ear-bones), where years of growth are laid down like the rings of a tree, as well as observations of individual fish in aquariums and other locations, give a maximum age of around 25 years: a lot, by fishy standards, and possibly only outdone by carp. A pike of 30 years or more is a rarity.

***

Kendal is moored mid-stream where the shallows begin to narrow abruptly towards the river mouth. Beneath him is the narrow channel carved by the ever-moving river water, six or maybe seven feet deep. Getting here, he has had one moment of excitement: a swirl on the calm surface behind the diving plug lure he has been towing. The worst thing a fisherman can do in such circumstances is slow down to allow the fish to catch up with the lure, for this inevitably perplexes them and makes them suspicious. He had dipped his oars in deeper, drawn on them harder, leaning back on each stroke to put some weight behind them. The sight of an escaping meal is maddening to a pike! But all he got for his effort, a few moments later, was another swirl, then the distinctive head and tail rise of a following sea-trout, albeit a good one, more interested in watching this curious creature, the twisting and diving lure, than in having a go at it.

The fish, losing interest, soon rose again a good deal further back and Kendal had been able to relax to his steady pace while he watched the fish van tootling along the shore road to pull up at the hotel to deliver fresh oysters, bass and lobster for the restaurant and more bait for him. Across the still loch he could clearly hear the driver's door open and, likewise the doors at the back. While the goods went inside the engine still ran, probably to keep the refrigeration going. Then the van had tootled off again after more door slamming while Kendal approached his position, lining up two bankside trees to one side and an alder and distant house to the other to put himself close to where his bait had lain yesterday. Then he quietly lowered the anchor.

He reels in the plug and snips it off then unclips the line spool on his reel to change it for one with a heavier line, 15lb breaking strain. Should he hook a very big pike, it will have plenty of open water to run in with no discernible snags to smash his tackle. He threads on the three-inch orange-topped white plastic float he used yesterday, and rummages in the bottom of his tackle bag to find half a matchstick which he fixes with a little hitch knot about 8ft up the line; it will stop the float in this position, meaning his bait can dangle - hopefully enticingly - just above the lake bed. A flying paternoster lead - a weight, a 2ft length of line and a tiny swivel - is next, then the business end, a wire trace, proof against all those sharp teeth, which has two sliding unbarbed treble hooks and a final stout unbarbed treble at the extreme end. It too is fixed to the line with a small steel swivel: a pike can kick and twist all it likes now without winding up the line so that it kinks, tangles and breaks.

He finds his plastic chopping-board stowed in the little bow locker and unpacks one bag of bait, the mackerel. He can feel the current from the river running under the keel but to test it he cuts the head off one of the fish, drops it over the side and watches it. There's enough movement in the flow to tumble it over and over as it sinks, falling steadily astern. A bit more flow than yesterday, perhaps, understandable with all that rain. Satisfied the spot will do, he continues to chop up the fish into chunks of an inch or so and drops them in the water one by one, smelling the sharp, oily tang of the flesh and curdled black blood as he does so: a scent trail for his quarry to follow all the way to the big bait, perhaps snacking on the way.

Unhurriedly, he picks up the other mackerel, slashes it twice on each flank so that its juices too will draw the monsters on, and starts to rig it up as a bait: one hook in the topmost treble is nicked through the thin neck of the fish's tail, round which he also makes one turn of the wire trace. To make doubly sure of fixing it here he overwraps this with a twist of red darning wool, tied tightly. With another turn of the wire trace around the fish he fixes the middle treble in its back, where the flesh is toughest. A final twist brings the end-hook neatly to the fish's head where it can be bitten securely into the strong gill plate. Now, when he lifts his rod, it dangles upside-down. While pike do not invariably swallow their prey head first they do so more often than not, so that protuberances like spines or hard fins to not stop it sliding down the gullet. Placed in the way they are, Kendal's hooks will also cause no obstruction, and will be points-upwards when he strikes to set them. Without more ado he lobs the baited rig ahead of the bow rope, towards the river mouth, lets the bale arm off the reel so that the line can run free, puts the rod end over the forward gunwale and then gently lifts his anchor far enough to allow the boat to drift slowly backwards. Fifty yards back he drops it again, and when the bogey wheel again holds the boat securely he gives it a little slack then ties up. All set. He re-engages the reel and takes up slack line. The tip of the orange float pops up obligingly, like a thumbs-up sign.

Now he can settle back, relax, wait. Only when he has finished his activities does he notice that the weather is on the change. The sky is still bright, but high up there's a grey misty skein of cloud, lacy, vague like a spider's web, and it's racing north-south. Very, very fast. Ahead of him, still at some distance, a black horizontal bar is growing and filling the gap between the two mountain peaks, and even as he looks the scrubby oaks and birches half a mile or more up the river glen have started to wave wildly, the last of their leaves scattering like confetti in an approaching squall.

Kendal feels a sudden temperature drop long before it hits the lake, and he zips his waterproof jacket up tightly under his chin. Barring a few of those irritating trickles that always seem to get in somewhere, he's pretty weatherproof. In his mind's eye as the sky begins to darken he can imagine a big pike picking up the scent trail he has laid, tasting a sample of the bigger treat laid out ahead. Perhaps just such a fish is headed upstream, passing near the boat at this very moment.

He's unaware, though, that one particular pike that he would be very pleased to catch is currently bound on another course, although if she completes her patrol she will eventually, inevitably come upon him and the trap he has laid, albeit from an unexpected direction. And there's a high possibility of extreme danger for one or even perhaps both of them in any encounter that ensues in this rendezvous...if anything happens at all, of course. That's fishing!

Chapter 6

Hunting through the shallows has not always been Lucie's preferred way of earning a living. In fact she's led an adventurous life, has travelled broadly within the confines of the loch, and has seen sights most humans will never see.

When she hatched from one of the many thousands of eggs her matriarch laid not far from the spot she today patrols, she was a tiny, rudimentary little transparent strip of a thing that didn't even have a proper mouth, let alone a fearsome set of jaws - just a sucker-like depression that allowed her to hold onto the stem of a water weed, dangling with all the other hatchlings, just like fruit hanging from a bough waiting to be plucked. And plucked they were, many of these little pike, all around her, by all manner of water creatures as well as other tiny and not-so-tiny fish: a share went to the tadpoles, a share to the water beetles and water scorpions, a share to the fearsome blood-sucking larvae of dragonflies and damsel flies, and not a tiny share to fish of her own kind, larger (but still small) pike. In the first few days while she consumed a tiny sac of yolk, which so far allowed her to live and develop without feeding, countless of Lucie's siblings perished. But then she developed a mouth and could swim free of the weed, look for jiggling little plankton creatures that would help her grow and daily become less and less of a target for opportunist snackers.

A natural species survival strategy lies in the over-production of offspring because of the vast numbers of them that perish in their early. If mother pike were to lay fewer eggs (and they lay up to 50,000 eggs to each kilogramme of their body weight), hardly any of the offspring would survive the high level of predation - and the few that did might lower the lake's gene pool. Conversely, if a lot of the offspring survived, they would find themselves ceaselessly fighting each other for a share of the available food and might actually deplete stocks severely. And then, like the Thackeray ditty about three sailors from Bristol City, who stole a ship and went to sea and quickly depleted the larder, as Gorging Jack said to Guzzling Jimmy, "there's nothing left...us must eat we!"

Anyone catching a glance of her in clear water at this point would indeed see poet Ted Hughes' *Pike, Perfect Pike*: amber-finned and beautifuly resplendent in leaf green and lemon yellow livery, lean and rakish, long-jawed and large-eyed, this little jewel is in every way an enamelled miniature of the adult she is destined to be. She is also ever on the alert for a possible meal. In fact, in these early years, it's the main drive of her life, 24-7 and in all seasons. She is so good at hunting that within a year she is almost a foot long, the scourge of other fish up to a quarter of her size and even a menace to those approaching half her size. She's already eaten several of her own kind.

Life so far has not been without its dangers. Several times she has very nearly become a meal for other, larger fish; a young web-footed otter once hunted her for a quarter of a mile along the shore while she squirmed in and out of reed-stems for cover, and it was only because it found something else that was easier to catch and eat that she got away. Once, stalking through pondweed, she was suddenly aware of a big eye peering down at her from above the surface, and moments later a long bill plunged down and speared a small perch she had been eyeing up for lunch. What she had thought to be a couple of nearby reed stems then revealed themselves as the legs of a great grey heron. And in midsummer a large brown bird had started to haunt the shallows, catching fish in hooked sickle talons and hauling them up into the air and back to a huge nest in a Scots pine on one of the islands. But like most fish, not just pike, she recovered quickly from these traumas and scrapes. In an eat or be eaten world, you just have to get on with things! Thus it is that you can sometimes catch a fish, throw it back, and catch it again within minutes.

***

Throughout the early period of her life, the shallows remain her happy hunting ground, but although the weeds here give good cover from spring to mid-December, there's a lean time afterwards when she has to find old reed stems and lily-root forests to skulk in if she wants to mount an ambush to fill her ever-hungry gut. But in the bitter January of her second year some of the other larger pike, she begins to notice, are heading away from the nursery area. She follows, curious and as usual ever-cautious, as they start to skirt along the lake shore. After a while she comes upon quite large gatherings of pike of all sizes in a series of shallow bays where the fine grit bed affords no purchase for weed roots. They are concentrated at the edge of a gravel shelf beyond which the water plunges into black-blue, immeasurable depths, and they all appear to be waiting.

With the approach of dusk there is a sudden stirring among her fellow predators, and then, in ones and twos at first, but in ever increasing numbers, ghostly grey shapes begin to emerge from the depths, some quite big - a foot or more long - but many smaller.

The hovering pike strike immediately, their waiting over, but they are soon overwhelmed by the sheer numbers of the powan - ancient whitefish - coming up from the depths they inhabit most of the year round and gathering on the gravel banks to spawn. With quivering bodies the female powan, black and silver in the moonlight, begin to shed what will soon become a storm of sticky eggs, the males swimming in among them and leaving trails of fertilising milt through the mass as it sinks to the gravel. Encouraged by the hormones and pheromones which soon lace the water, the powan pay no heed to the gorging pike but carry on with their mating frenzy. The pike, including Lucie, feed at will of course - it is in their nature - but there are limits even to the amount a pike may swallow and digest in one go.

Night after night the feast went on, sometimes continuing in daylight. Other species came along to eat not the fish, but the oil-rich eggs left by these mysterious visitors from the deep, trout and perch taking their fill too. But then, one day, it was all over; just a few stragglers appeared from the deep, while those that had not been eaten retreated to their abysses in the vast lake, as if they had never been there at all. The spawning season had ended.

***

Rather than retrace her way back to familiar weedy shallows after the feasting, Lucie continued her exploration of the other regions of the lake. It was vast, but she was encouraged to carry on because there never seemed to be any real shortage of food wherever she strayed - though never on the same scale as the powan spawning frenzy. Mostly she was eating small silver fish - mainly roach and dace fry – but also small, stripy rough-scaled perch whose spiny defensive dorsal fins were of no consequence to her. With her ever-expanding size, in girth as well as length, and a wicked trap of a mouth that widened and lengthened in proportion, she could tackle bigger and bigger fish, and occasionally when roach were scarce and powan were not available, she'd add a trout or two to her diet, even small salmon, and - of course - other pike.

She found many inlets similar to the one in which she had been born, and there were weed-free ones too like the powan breeding bay, but in some places the land fell away sheer into the water, much deeper than she felt comfortable with for the time being. All fish are vulnerable to sudden attacks from below, usually by bigger fish but sometimes from a clever otter which has perfected the art of surprise.

She discovered also many islands in her perambulation - again, some were steep-sided, others surrounded by shallows. If she liked a place enough and didn't have to work too hard for her food, she would often stay for a while. Invariably, dwindling numbers of prey fish would drive her on, or in the summer concentrations of boat activity, men, women and children splashing in the water, larking around. She had no fear of these activities - why would they worry her? - but they did tend to drive away the smaller fish on which she depended.

One or two boats would also make their way quietly to the more secluded parts of the lake and stay there for the day, only returning as darkness fell. One of these was to give her the shock of her life. Feeling peckish one day, she'd followed through the water a peculiar set of vibrations which she felt sure was a fish behaving oddly - and a fish behaving oddly is usually injured or ill and therefore easy meat. Nearing the source, she looked up and ahead to see a trout which appeared to be dancing on the surface, half in and half out, and strangely it was making its way steadily towards the boat. By now all her hunting instincts were in play and she'd made up her mind that she was going to nail this oddity. Following it almost to the boat, she fairly whistled at it from below, jaws opening wide...

But instead of seizing a juicy young trout, Lucie found herself biting on a strong, weed-like mesh which at that very moment was being lifted from the water, the trout on one side and she on the other. Amazed, she hung on momentarily to the netting. Most of her head was hauled out of the water, and a man loomed above, looking down at her, his jaw dropping with surprise. Her alarm bell started to ring loudly and two things happened simultaneously - she let go and fell back in the water, while the fisherman fell violently back into his boat with a resounding clonk, along with the trout. Losing a meal like this made her furiously angry, and she swam three or four times round the boat glaring at the fisherman while he glared back. But after a while, since the trout hadn't reappeared, she swam of to find another meal. You can be sure the fisherman recounted this story on returning to his friends, no doubt with a little suitable adornment, especially regarding Lucie's size!

At the start of her third year, Lucie was surprised to find herself in very familiar territory; shallow, mud-bottomed and still bearing vestiges of summer weed. She recognised too the taste of fresh snow-tasting water coming from the nearby river mouth. She had completely circumnavigated the lake! However, now was not the time to linger because her memory told her this was the time of year to join the throngs waiting for the powan to re-emerge from the deep and spawn on the gravels. So on she went, starting circuit two. And once again she fed to her fill in the spawning bay, moving on when the powan mating ritual was over. But it was not the end of her acquaintance with these blue-silver fish for that year. However, there was still plenty to preoccupy her before that.

One warm, dark night, gliding alert at the roadside edge of the loch, she'd skirted a small bay where there were lots of lights, men and women shouting. Then there was a splash; something had been thrown into the water not far behind her. She turned on her tail to investigate: a large black package was sinking, slowly, and whatever was in it was fighting for air, kicking, struggling to get out. As the package moved less and less, and then sank completely below the surface, the lights on the shore went out abruptly and a vehicle drove off, its vibrations dwindling in the night. And after a minute or two movement in the package ceased...but that wasn't the first dead human she had seen. The species didn't seem to be at all happy under the water! She'd once seen one, a young woman, just walk into the water and keep on walking, neither bothering to swim nor try to reach air when her head went beneath the waves; for a time she had floated at the surface, face down,hair spreading out, a bizarre sight. Then she sank slowly to the bed where a gallery soon gathered: small fish, eels, hordes of water-lice. Within a few days they'd started to nibble, nibble relentlessly until, quite suddenly, a rope and grapple thrown from the shore plunged and snagged the woman's clothing and she was dragged to the side and away. Pity, thought Lucie, who had already eaten few of the nibblers, it had been getting to be quite a busy little area...

Just below the village on her home shore were the skeletal remains of two men, lying not far from one another, while almost adjacent to her nursery ground lay a huge winged machine which had fallen out of the sky long before her birth, its skeleton pilot's thumb bone still pressed against the cannon firing button. But Lucie's most bizarre find by far was at the far end of the loch, where it again narrowed to a river which in this case flowed out of the broad water and on down to the sea. Here, just emerging from the mud and in a long, long slowly fossilising boat sat the skeltons of twelve men in full armour, almost as if they would row away from the spot if given an order to do so. They were ancient; wrapped in preservative bindings, the warriors and the proudly-crowned king at the prow had their feet among the royal treasures, and before being cast out into the loch the boat had been set on fire. Odd creatures, men.

Odd too, she would soon discover, were powan.

***

The year had moved well beyond spring and, with the water warming rapidly, she was about two thirds of her way round the loch. For no obvious reason, she had struck a period of bounty: plenty of roach and perch to feed upon and almost no competition from other pike. Where had they all gone?

For some of the rapidly-shortening nights now, however, she had been picking up strange vibrations from far out in the open water, over the so-far unexplored deeps. What was going on out there? Was it anything to do with the disappearing pike? One particularly warm and clear night in early summer with a bright half moon high to the east, and with the odd vibrations seeming not too far distant, she was tempted to go and find out. And what she found

39

would have a major influence on her future size.

It felt really peculiar to leave the reassurance of the loch's shoreline behind and strike out into the unknown, the water growing deeper all the while. All the same, she had the moon for reference, and she knew most of the predators that were a threat to her would not be about after dusk. After a while the water, which had been clear so far, started first to become misty, then downright murky. With her wonderful big eyes she could see that she was entering a cloud of fantastic little creatures of all shapes and sizes, tiny plants too: plankton, masses of it, welled up from below. Then she jumped; in the murk she had nearly bumped into a hovering pike, a fish much bigger than herself. A little way on there was another, of about the same size. They just hung there, inactive, gills working slowly, ticking over. Were they waiting for something? If so, what? Minutes later, her questions were answered. She heard a sound like a flock of birds, all whistling and whispering to one another, and then out of the miasma and across the border of her forward circle of vision swam the leading edge of a vast shoal of fish, all busily sip-feeding at the surface. And from one side, silvered by moonlight, she saw the flank of a huge pike turn unhurriedly, rise to the edge of the shoal, pluck one fish away and sink while it turned its prey to swallow it head first. Meanwhile the huge shoal moved on, oblivious to the loss and apparently endless.

Other pike began to rise all around her to pluck from the shoal, and not to be outdone Lucie followed their example: powan! It was those powan again!

For all its considerable size the powan shoal was actually not endless, but after it had moved on there was another shoal, and then another. A whole succession of them swam past while Lucie and her fellow pike ate to their fill without effort, and the moon moved across its semi-circle of the heavens and dawn grew closer and closer.

When the moon had slipped behind the glen ridge top and there was no more than a hint of extra light to the east, the water began to clear suddenly. The plankton were sinking, and with them the powan shoals, feeding on the clouds of tiny creatures as they sank deeper and deeper into the dark blue abyss and away from approaching sunlight. Unsure what to do next, and certainly not at all hungry, Lucie hovered for a moment above this descending mass: then she noticed she was almost alone - some of the other pike were following the powan down, sinking with them as they dropped and dropped.

And down she went too. Fine bubbles of air sped past her on the way to the surface as pike and powan adjusted and tuned their buoyancy bladders to allow for a steady descent; she was in free-fall through a green-blue bubble-world, and all the while the pressure increased, especially on her already-tight flanks. It grew darker and darker as they went, although by now up above the sun had already peered over the eastern ridges. Still they sank, predators and prey, on and on.

Now and then, even as they descended, a pike would be tempted again and would help itself to a nearby powan. And by degrees some of the pike, especially the smaller ones like herself, stopped their descent and rested, hovering, although ever-alert. But Lucie went on down, down, down with the powan, just because some of the other pike were still doing so and she wanted to know why. And then finally, at heaven only knows what depth, it all stopped. They had reached the very bottom. The cloud of plankton spread itself out across the silt, some of the creatures burying themselves and others forming a densely packed layer on which the powan still fed steadily. The sheer amount of powan here was vast and so concentrated that they were jostling her sides. And the pike that remained among them (if they had not been there already) were very big indeed. Lucie found herself among giants!

Once she had acclimatised herself to this always-dark and highly pressurised world, she found the living very easy indeed. With every nightfall, the clouds of plankton would begin to rise towards the lake surface, and some of the powan - and the pike - would go with them. However, the larger pike, the real juggernauts, would stay: there were fish enough staying in these deeps to give them all the food they wanted without the tedious business of adjusting swim bladders every night to follow the rising hordes. The powan that stayed behind tended to be larger, older and by definition slower fish; easy pickings. Sick fish also stayed, unless they had fallen victim to a strange parasite which gave them whirling disease, dooming them to swim round and round in circles on the surface of the water until some hungry bird picked them off (carrying on the parasite's bizarre life cycle). And dying and dead fish sank to these regions, and to a pike, food is food whether it's dead or alive. While she was wary of the very large pike around her at first, when it became clear they were simply not interested in any other food than powan, Lucie became more relaxed in her new surroundings. She had a choice, each night, of rising to feed on the surface shoals or staying. More and more often she found staying the easier option, with occasional forays to follow the powan up to the shallows during their breeding season.

And if it hadn't been for an irrational but irresistible urge to revisit her nursery grounds, there she might have stayed. Whether or not she ever questioned why the urge was so strong, when this chasm that was so bountiful and also weather-proof against a bitter winter and not much better spring above, we shall never know. But she had to go. Had to.

41

Chapter 7

When he first saw Mab, Kendal had to make a move. Had to.

She was working in The Battery, which was the name given to the row of telephones with a line of seated women animatedly calling advertisers to cajole them into taking space in the next issue of the Bristol paper that had given him his first job. Nearly all these women were young and pretty, and certainly highly attractive to a young man with his foot on the first rung of the ladder. But Mab stood out from the crowd at first sight.

Sitting at the newsdesk (he was later to move to sub-editors when it was realised his English was better than most), he could not stop his eyes being drawn to her in the glass-enclosed section at the far end of the large partitioned storeroom the newspaper staff shared. They all of them sat in rooms high above the thundering brass-reeled press which lurked in the basement garage, reeking of ink, hot lead and engine oil. Mab had tightly curled black hair, cut fairly short, freckles, and, under viciously plucked eyebrows and vastly extended lashes, the most vivid blue eyes he had ever seen.

He had yet to discover her dazzling smile or even her name, since he spent most of his time in the office wondering how she managed to pass entire days without ever looking his way (even though this would have, undoubtedly, meant acute embarrassment for him, had it happened). Other lads had their eyes on her too although, so far as he knew, nobody had plucked up enough courage to ask her for a date. His chance came one day when, given a half-hour break, he found her alone in the canteen eating a cheese roll - everybody in the industry worked odd shifts, out of kilter not only with the outside world but also with one another. Under the circumstances it would have been rude not to join her, or at least ask if she minded. Plucking up courage he did so. She fluttered mascara-heavy eyelids and responded with a brilliant wide smile and in an instant he was lost. Completely.

"Be my guest."

He fought back shyness.

"I'm Mark...Mark Kendal.   I've seen you in the battery."

"Mabel. But you can call me Mab. I've seen you too. You're a reporter."

He was actually an apprentice reporter...press jobs were like that, just after the war, you learned on the job. You didn't have to go to university to earn your ticket. And jobs of all kinds that did not demand a degree were plentiful.

"Will be, I hope. Well, a journalist, anyway. A sub-editor, probably."

An awkward silence followed and they both looked away, but found their eyes drawn back to each other. She glanced at the little jewelled watch on her freckled arm, and tapped it pointedly.

"I have to be back in a mo. Running out of time."

He grasped at the lead, wondering how he'd managed to muster up the daring.

"Can I...can I see you?"

Kendal had clearly read the prompt accurately.

"I don't know - can you?" she said, standing - a joke. It let them both laugh, broke the tension.

"A drink in the Lion over the road after work. For starters."

She nodded and left him with his own untouched roll and tea. Hopefully there would be other courses to follow.

***

The following Christmas Eve saw them marry in a hurry at a register office: Mab was pregnant. By that time they had moved on after he qualified and were living together in a tiny flat in Leeds, not far from the cricket ground. The new paper had been glad to snap them up as a pair that 'knew the trade', but it was clear Mab would soon have to give up her job. As two fly-the-nests since school, both had only tenuous links to their parents who did not attend the ceremony - parents who had survived a bitter war were well aware of the needs of young people to act precipitously. Mab's people lived in north London, Kendal's to the south of Birmingham (he'd been one of four, two boys, two girls, born barely a year apart). They hadn't been told of the pregnancy but they probably guessed. The only people at the wedding were a couple of work colleagues.

They weren't prepared for the miscarriage in February. It nearly wrecked the relationship but it hung together somehow. The following February Jenny was born with no complications. They had also met one another's families, adding to the cement which kept them together along with a deeper love from the shared disappointment of their earlier loss. When Jenny was born they were still living at the Headington flat behind the main road supermarket but with a little help from Kendal's parents they managed a deposit on a terrace house in Chapeltown - a poor area, But then you had to start somewhere. Instead of settling down, however, it made them discover they still had itchy feet. It was time to move on.

Thus Jenny's school years were spent in Plymouth, but when she earned herself a university place, albeit in relatively nearby Exeter, Kendal announced out of the blue to Mab: "You know, I've been feeling for some time that I'd like to get back to my roots again. Look at the old places I used to know, where I went fishing, that sort of thing."

Mab took it calmly, though it must have seemed they were now firmly settled in the Westcountry. She also read his thoughts pretty accurately.

"Move again, you mean?"

"Not necessarily," he said evasively. "Just to have a poke around, that sort of thing."

***

They had a car, a thrifty Ford. 'Poking around' started out with the odd trip up the A38 but quickly turned into a series of house hunting expeditions. And a job interview. In hardly any time at all, it seemed, they were moving again.

At first Kendal had been surprised and a little dismayed by the amount of development, mainly housing but also some light industrial units, in and around his old home. Up to now they had looked in once or twice to see his parents, and then to bury his father and, within a few months, his mother. By then only Mab still had her mother alive. But while some of the old places were buried irretrievably in bricks and concrete, gems still remained, as well as his old street, just round the corner from where they acquired their new home. And much of the old Brightwell estate, now a leading health, residential and care home complex, was still intact - including his old fishing lake set like a jewel in its midst.

One bright October day found him standing where he'd once stood with two school companions on the steep wooded bank looking down on the water. Keen-eyed, he found the shadow of a stalking pike, quite a good one, not far from the spot of his first pike capture.

Although he had enjoyed a fishing session from time to time throughout their life as a family, once back on home territory Kendal wasted no time in taking up his old love on a more regular basis. He found it a useful antidote to stressful newspaper work, and began to indulge himself as regularly as some of his colleagues indulged themselves on their favourite golf courses. Mab, glad of his new-found happiness, sometimes accompanied him on longer trips, exploring nearby towns until it was time to pick him up again. A few years passed in this way, as years will, until one day Kendal came home from a pike fishing session down on Chew Valley Lake, south of Bristol, and announced: "Mab, I think I know where I can catch a record pike."

He'd had not only a good trip, catching a 30lb pike and two smaller ones, but a revelation: suddenly he saw why the pike in the reservoir were in general much bigger than fish found elsewhere. And when he finished thinking deeply about why this should be so, his conclusion had implications far beyond the shores of Chew Valley.

"Good," she said. "You'll be famous then."

Kendal laughed, fully aware he was being humoured.

Fame was not the objective: an obsession had just been born.

***

The campervan, small but reliable and with low mileage (at least when he had bought it!) made the Scottish trips cheaper and more practical than getting there by any other means and paying for expensive accommodation. It was also useful for summer touring holidays with Mab. After a while, Kendal settled into a regular early winter trip north on his own, and when his retirement came he had been able to extend two-week trips to four or even five weeks away at a time. What made this considerably easier was the fact Jenny and her husband, Mike, had also moved back to their area, and she and Mab spent a lot of time together.

Kendal bought a boat - glass resin, LOA 3.66m, beam 1.37m, mid-ship depth 0.55m - in short, a 12ft runabout. He rescued it from a caravan yard, where it looked unwanted, forlorn and neglected, for a bargain price, along with a little two-wheel trailer to carry it. He had the van fitted with a towbar. The obsession grew.

***

In one sense fishing, or rather 'angling' with a rod and line (to make a distinction of the gentle art) is all about obsession. Non-fishermen can make many mistakes about angling born of ignorance: for a start, a true 'angler' never fishes for the pot, although a trout fisherman or a sea fisherman might provide the odd supper from their catch. Most fish, and particularly 'coarse' fish (ie not 'game' fish like trout and salmon) go back whence they came, and are gently replaced rather than unceremoniously chucked in. Worthy adverseries demand respect. Neither are fishermen forever in a state of mindless inertia when they are on the riverbank or sitting in a boat, for all they might appear to be so in some instances. Few of them will not know what they want to catch, both in terms of species and size of fish, and most will have calculated the bait or lure and the method of fishing it that will help them achieve their objective.

Concentration is paramount to success: a 'bite' or take can sometimes be no more than a minute deviation of the line that a float is moving with the current downriver, or a little twitch of the rod-tip. The reaction to this has to be immediate, in many cases, so alertness is also essential.

The word 'interactive' is much used these days, and is usually linked with computer or game-console activities, but fishermen have always been highly interactive with their surroundings - while watching for significant signs of fish, such as a trail of small bubbles or a moorhen giving a lily-patch a wide berth, they are immersed in the flow of life all about them, a part of its reality. Stay still enough, and a kingfisher may settle on your rod as if it is just another bankside twig; make an unwary move or tread too heavily, and every nearby fish will scoot for a mile. In no time at all, a fisherman feels himself becoming part of the matrix.

Not many fishermen are driven by a desire to break records. In fact, while most would be happy if a record trout or roach came along, the most nearly all anglers aspire to is a good day or night's fishing. And if you catch nary a fish, there's contentment in the fact that you've been trying and usually consolation in the enjoyment derived from your surroundings. Camaraderie too - not all anglers are loners like Kendal.

Neither are fishermen completely oblivious of the cares and worries they bring along from their everyday lives. However, the change of environment and emphasis often allows them new perspectives on whatever is on their minds. Often this is helpful. Very occasionally there's a revelation!

Fish or no fish, angling is always rewarding and unwinding: it embodies the true sense of the word 'recreation', particularly for the stressed or those who lead busy and complex lives.

***

So, the start of Lucie's fourth year: it began with an urge to quit the easy living of preying on the obligingly plentiful powan shoals, and return to the area in which she had hatched. Gradually, almost unnoticeably, her body had been changing all winter, ahead of this prompting. Long sacs of egg cells in her body cavity were starting to mature and new hormones flooded her senses. She became dreamy, and not a bit interested in food, but at the same time she moved into the shallows with quiet assurance.

***

The weedy area is extensive and there is ample room for many female pike, some of them extremely large, deep-bodied and packed with eggs, to share the space without impinging on one another's territory. And from nowhere, it seems, each of these females has in train a shoal of male admirers, from five or six apiece but sometimes up to 20 or more. And they're inevitably a quarrelsome lot, encouraged by the attractor pheromones released into the water by the females to spar for her attention. Inevitably, too, some bear many battle scars before they have sorted out an order, the strongest and fittest (but not necessarily the biggest) getting the chance to sidle up alongside the female until they lie eye to eye. Behind her as she goes deeper into the weed forest, Lucie notices she has half a dozen suitors of her own, all of different sizes, including a giant of twice her own length. Yet while the boys are happy quarrelling among themselves, they too have stopped eating. Lucie feels no real threat, even from the big one, but she is never completely unwary.

Strong evolutionary forces are in play. Male pike grow more slowly, attain smaller maximum sizes and live less than half as long as females. A big female finds it suits her to have a smaller male alongside as she starts to lay eggs. It ensures that the milt he sheds is wafted back through her falling spawn as he flexes his tail. He is certain to run out of milt, exhausted, long before she stops shedding her massive cache of eggs over several days. As he drops out of the picture another male comes alongside to take his place, and so it goes on.

Lucie is glad when she loses her largest follower. She had a feeling the match would be an unsuitable one. And perhaps the fickle male, on the trail of a much larger female, realised the same thing. That left her with just a handful of smaller admirers, who did their duty while she came to terms with the new experience of squeezing little batches of eggs, a dozen or so at a time, from her body. Sticky, the eggs tumbled down into the weed and lodged there, where emerging embryos would have some cover to protect them.

Still only a relatively small pike, she had expelled all her eggs by the middle of the second day. The males faded away back into the weeds. She felt bruised, exhausted. And, after two more days, ravenously hungry.

Lucie set off to hunt anew, having fulfilled her obligations to the species. Behind, in each fertilised egg, wriggled a tiny transparent tadpole of a thing. If these little scraps of life got through their early days unscathed as she had done, they would carry some amazing genetic coding - particularly the females, which had the potential to live long, to grow large and, above all, to survive.

***

When the potato incident had come up, Kendal remembered that Jenny had remarked a little while ago that "mum was a bit strange today". Pressed on what she'd meant, she had been unable to put it into words.

The gist of it, however, was that Mab had repeated a couple of things as if she hadn't already mentioned them a couple of minutes earlier, leaving Jenny baffled.

But they only discussed this event in passing, because Jenny had problems of her own; namely, there had been a falling out between her and husband Mike. All couples have their disagreements from time to time but to Kendal it seemed more than a small thing that Mike had gone back to stay with his parents, who had a large country house, to "think about things for a while". It's one thing to separate to clear the air but to abandon your wife when she has just learned she is pregnant with your child looked a good deal more serious.

Also to Kendal, who came from a generation which had been trained for independence and had longed to achieve as early as possible, this flight of Mike's to his family didn't seem very adult. Surely, he thought initially, you worked through problems yourself, made your own decisions. But all the same he knew that later generations than his own depended for longer on their parents than had been the case in his young days, and indeed often lived 'at home' for a lot of their early adult life. And, when he thought about it, he and Mab would be glad to welcome back Jenny and their forthcoming grandchild should the occasion demand. For the moment though it was just an uneasy situation which could go one way or the other.

"It worries me dad - I've always been on good terms with Joe and Mary and I can still phone up and talk to them, but at times it's a bit frosty. And often Mike isn't there, or at least they say he isn't there. 'Down the pub' comes up quite often. And I still don't know what I've done, except to say I want to stay where I am when junior is born."

"And he doesn't - is that all that this is about?"

She didn't answer immediately, so Kendal guessed he might have put his finger on it - the couple lived just around the corner, and Jenny and Mab were pretty close. Mike's family lived near Exeter.

"I guess that's the root of it," she said eventually. "He went down there for an interview and he didn't tell me he was going. The last straw was when he started showing me all these house details from estate agents on the internet. Look, dad, I'm happy here and I think it would be a mistake to go now. I've got all the pre-natal stuff lined up for a start. And we've got a nice house - a bit small but we don't need more for now. He's got a good enough job as well. I just think it would be a real upheaval to move right now - and mum will be such a big help when it happens."

Up to that point, he'd put the little worry about Mab out of mind, at least to one side.

***

After the diagnosis Mab's decline had been swift, unbelievably disappointing, demoralising. The term 'dementia', Kendal quickly learned, covered not just the most well-known form of the disease, Alzheimers, but also vascular dementia, in which the patient suffered small strokes that shut off various parts of the brain and, consequently, some of the functions they performed. Mab had Alzheimers.

By degrees Kendal gently took over all the domestic and clerical duties which they had shared before. Mab remained cheerful in the early period, and although it was frequently explained to her that she had to accept a growing level of care, she steadfastly refused to believe that she was any different from the person she had always been.

"I don't see what all the fuss is about. I'm fine," was often her response. "Maybe a bit forgetful. It's allowed at my age."

Just how forgetful she was getting was brought home to Kendal one day when he'd tapped her on the shoulder in the garden to attract her attention. "What do you want?" she'd said sharply. "Who are you?" The light of recognition was slow to spread over her face...

Two small strokes which literally floored her had followed. With the first, after a desperate struggle, Kendal had managed to get her up and into a chair, her sheer weight bringing home to him for the first time two things: one, she was growing quite large, and two, it had been very hard to get her up again without help. The second time she fell, he gave up trying to lift her and called paramedics in. She'd had to be taken to the local A and E to check if the fall had done any physical damage. In a conversation with the hospital registrar he'd been asked if he had ever considered a permanent care home for her.

***

"Why don't you do some more of your Scottish trips, dad?"

It was Jenny who suggested he should start over again on his mission, get away from the house as well as the care home which he visited regularly.

"I'll be here to keep an eye on things, after all, and I promise I'll visit mum as often as I can."

It was a wrench but he did it. And while he still carried a lot of his cares on his shoulders on the long drive north, the fishing provided the respite he so desperately needed.

***

After the powan discovery Lucie settled into a pattern of life that changed little for several years. In spring, after mating and resting for a few days to recover, she made her way to the deep regions of the lake and let herself sink. In the depths, among the obliging powan, she had all she needed not just to sustain her but to let her grow far more rapidly than would be the case if she had remained an active hunter of the shallows. It was also less dangerous - no predators save her fellow pike could reach these depths since all were air breathers and, in any event, would never adapt to the severe water pressure. True some of the very large pike could have made a meal of her in the early days, but with the abundance of docile powan they had little interest in taking on anything that might prove difficult to catch and eat. And as she herself grew to proportions that would pop any fisherman's eyes, the likelihood of suffering an attack from her fellow creatures became less and less likely.

Once down, here she became a permanent resident except for her once-a-year expeditions to breed. She stayed even while some of the powan made their way up to their breeding grounds in the early spring, and in summer when they followed the plankton cloud up to the surface to enjoy the moonlight and warmth of a brief Scottish night. At this depth the temperature

49

remained fairly constant, even if it became fairly warm above, from where she could hear the occasional murmur of boat engines, and even when the first bitter winds of winter took the last of the leaves off the trees and blew them over the water surface like flotillas of little sailing ships. When the still long nights set in, and water in the bays froze, she still had a comfortable and easy life, using up little energy while echoes from the village boys throwing stones across the frozen water came down to her like sharp explosions in a vast and empty deep blue cavern.

And so it might have remained, but for the folly of man, and the desirability of her own kind as a target for fishermen. Large pike had always been caught in the loch, but the consistency with which it produced fish of around 30lb made it more and more popular, especially with specialist pike-anglers. In the late 1970s and 1980s hundreds flocked to try their luck in this prodigious big-pike water, and a particularly widespread method of going after them was live-baiting: a small fish, very much alive-o, trammelled with vicious arrays of anchor-like strong treble hooks and dangling beneath a float big enough to stop it being dragged under by the actions of the bait alone (not, it might be noted, a method Kendal nowadays agreed with).

To save themselves the time and trouble of having to catch bait fish when they arrived at the loch, many fishermen brought live fish in buckets with them, caught from their home waters. A favourite bait species was ruffe (alternative name 'pope'), a small and fairly drab member of the perch family - plentiful in many of the east Midlands rivers and canals and some northern English waters. Some of these fish were lucky enough to escape their restraining hooks and flee into the loch to recover, but many more which were left over were simply tipped in when the time came for the fishermen to pack up and go home. What the anglers who brought them either overlooked or simply did not know was that ruffe have a singular vice, if such it can be called - their favourite food, which they can gorge in large quantities, is the eggs of other fish. Second favourite is the larval fish which hatch from any eggs that remain!

Pause a moment, however, to pity the poor ruffe. Its heavily armed dorsal fin has in the past led to it being very badly treated, as Frank Buckland details in *The Natural History of British Fishes* (1880): "A cruel habit, which probably originated in some idea connected with Roman Catholic persecution, is practised up and down the Thames and, I believe, almost all over England. A wine cork is pressed tightly on to the spine of the dorsal fin. and the fish is turned loose; this is what is called 'plugging a pope'." Buckland goes on to describe how Midlands working men often dotted the waters on which they fished weekend matches with hundreds of these hapless corked fish. "A funny sight," to see the corked fish bobbing down the river, he concludes.

The effect of the released ruffe, which went on to breed rapidly, was devastating for the loch's resident fish species and the powan in particular. From the mid-1980s onwards they tore into the carpets of spawn on the powan breeding grounds. As a result, former interlopers ruffe are today one of the commonest species of the loch while powan are so rare that it is illegal to set out to catch one and the species has been excluded from the fishing record lists in the hope that nobody will kill any and perhaps those that remain have a chance of survival. Meanwhile, even local schoolchildren have been engaged in a captive powan breeding and rearing programme that may one day see fry large enough to escape predation returned to the loch. Some have also been moved to other Scottish lochs and reservoirs which previously did not contain powan and are free of ruffe - in some cases they appear to be thriving. And it has also been learned that they lend themselves to being farmed, though this takes them a long way from being a wild native fish of the loch, and one on which other fish have depended heavily. As for getting rid of the ruffe...well, there's a problem that may never be solved, like removing rabbits from Australia or eradicating Japanese knotweed!

Chapter 8

Like her fellow pike, Lucie did not at first notice the steady decline of the powan. By degrees, however, and over a few years, she became aware a meal in the depths was becoming harder and harder to find, and competion for anything that could be caught was fierce. Used to a lazy life of picking and choosing what she wanted to eat, with interludes of inactivity and digesting in between, the new lifestyle of constantly prowling, grabbing and bickering was starting to become unsettling. She was by now huge - much larger than the 30lb benchmark weight most pike fishermen would call a big fish. Her back was broad and long, and her flanks deep, and living for a long time away from sunlit meadows of weeds with shoals of colourful prey fish had given her a silvery sheen. In spite of her long period of relative inactivity she was superbly fit. To this giant among giants, it was becoming increasingly clear it was time to move on.

***

Since his wife had been in the care home Kendal had been doubly attentive, perhaps, in truth, getting in the way a bit of the care staff's routines as he made his daily visits. Going north again to fish was a wrench - whether or not Mab recognised him (and she often did not) he felt comfort in being with her, and from time to time he had the bitter-sweet reward of her smile. But he found the break away to Scotland refreshing and sustaining through the year that followed.

And this was his second year, his second attempt in this particular place to put all the theory into practice and get on terms with an unseen adversary he somehow knew was there, somewhere. Along the wet and grimy road north there had been some change in him, however, and he realised he'd started thinking even more about what lay ahead than what lay behind.

His thoughts were not at this stage very optimistic. It wasn't just Mab's deteriorating condition that still occupied him. His own health remained a matter for concern. Shortly after Mab had moved into Bethlehem House, he'd grown more and more aware that the worrying trends in his behaviour would just not go away.

At first he had put this down to loneliness. The house, which until now had been living space for two people, had suddenly become half-empty: we fit ourselves around the people we live with, and they with us. If they are not there, we still make allowances for the spaces they occupied, as if they were still around. It takes a long time to start intruding, trespassing, taking short cuts. In the first few weeks, indeed months of living alone he would willingly have taken Mab back, whatever her condition. All that stopped him was one overriding thought that he was doing this for her own good. The myriad bits of help she needed for everyday existence, the hair-combing, tooth-brushing, nail clipping, toilet and washing mundanities, had gradually become unmanageable for her, and trying to cope with this had only highlighted his own inadequacies as a carer - let alone the worry that his strength and personal resources would be tested to the limit by a real emergency should she fall or suffer a stroke. Neither did they have the financial resources to install such care in their home in the form of an agency carer or nurse. If only they'd been more provident for this sort of thing!

So - once she had gone to stay among the patient nuns and carers - there he was in an empty house, expecting every moment to bump into her whenever he opened a door or went upstairs, or whenever he heard queer little noises like the creaks and clonks which all houses manage to produce when it's otherwise quiet. If he thought about all this for too long he became profoundly sad and was even moved to tears. It was at times almost as if she had died. Perhaps she had in a way.

***

"Don't forget your card."

A bag of shopping in each hand, he turned back to the checkout girl. Surely he hadn't left his bank card in the keypad? He had, though.

"Thanks," he said blushing and giving the rest of the queue at the till an apologetic smile. "Daft old bugger - I'd forget my head if it wasn't screwed on."

Then there had been a missed appointment at the dentist - perhaps not as serious as losing a debit card - and in coming home one day he found himself trying to unlock his front door with the electronic car key fob. A whole string of similar examples of absent-mindedness followed. At first this had all been mildly amusing and on occasions like the supermarket incident, slightly toe-curling. He'd even coined a name for it, putting it down to age: 'slippage'. It went along with not hearing people properly - for example, he was once quite sure he heard a woman who was chatting to a companion walking along the pavement in front of him: "I must go back to the moon sometime - I haven't been there for ages." In the hope they might actually be extra-terrestials he'd made an effort to overtake and examine them, but they proved disappointingly normal. Yet perhaps he'd heard correctly after all and 'the moon' was a restaurant or a pub or something like that? Other instances of mis-hearing followed - they were occasionally whimsical, even amusing, but mostly disconcerting.

By degrees, however, it all started to get worrying. So much so that he asked his GP, Brian Cox, for his views on the subject - introducing the matter during an appointment to have his ears looked at and possibly syringed to improve his hearing.

"First things first," said the relatively young doctor who had taken over at the surgery three years earlier. To Kendal, he was still on trial. "There is nothing wrong with your ears pysically - a bit of wax but nothing to worry about. At your age, however, it wouldn't be uncommon to start losing some of the hearing tones - the sharpness if you like. I wouldn't bother with hearing aids yet, however - see how you get along and come back in six months' time if you're still worried. And as for the other matter...'slippage' you called it? That's a very good word, but I don't think I've come across it in my books. Not a recognised condition, unless my education is lacking."

A pause. Was he going to brush that off too, patronising young bastard?

"Your wife...Mrs Kendal has dementia, right? And you are worried you might also have the same problem. I'm sure you realise it isn't catching, but that said there's no reason you shouldn't contract Alzheimers. It's a little early for your age but I wouldn't say unknown, though I would say that worry and stress might well be a big part of your problem. A lot on your mind, perhaps?"

Kendal nodded. It couldn't be denied. "Maybe."

Cox turned to his computer screen, and Kendal admired how ably he rattled the keyboard without looking at what his fingers were doing. Deft. That was young people for you - he'd probably never even seen a clattery mechanical typewriter, except perhaps in period films.

"There," he said turning back. "I've asked our cognitive assessment specialist to give you an appointment. He has clinics at this surgery and you'll either hear from his secretary or get something in the post."

"So you think..." Kendal began. The doctor shook his head and smiled.

"No I don't think what you'r thinking, not at all. But we'd better make sure and it'll be reassuring for you. Try not to worry so much - Mrs Kendal is in good hands, you know."

Five weeks later Kendal found himself being ushered into a consulting room by the ever-smiling Dr Ran. With an all-pervading sense of *deja vu*, he was asked by the consultant psychiatrist to remember some words, and then given a series of paper tests - arranging words, shapes, that sort of thing.

"Good," said Dr Ran at the end of their intereview, cocking his head on one side. "And can you remember the words I gave to you at the start?"

He could.

"Just as I thought - a great deal on your mind. We try to deal with many things at the same time, and usually this is just not possible. You are not sleeping well?"

Not well at all, said Kendal. Wakeful periods in the middle of the night while he reviewed all his problems were frequent. A comforting cup of tea and a biscuit sometimes helped to switch him off, give an hour or so's sleep towards dawn.

"Aha," said the good doctor, worry was probably at the root of his problems. Did he have a hobby, some way to relax? Oh yes, Kendal told him.

"Fishing...that sounds rather good to me," said Dr Ran. "But just to make sure I can arrange for a scan at the General Hospital. It's very quick and it'll show if there's any build-up of plaque that might cause problems. If anything it'll probably put your mind at rest. And as for sleep, I suggest you leave anything work-related out of the bedroom. If you wake, just concentrate on your breathing - in and out, in and out. That can be very calming."

A mind at rest would be just the ticket, Kendal though as he left clutching yet another appontment card.

And quick the scan was, as promised - no more than a couple of minutes lying on his back with his head in a giant tube, a buzz and a click and it was all over.

"I'm afraid that's as exciting as it gets," said the woman technician, switching off the machinery. "We'll forward the pictures to Dr Ran and you'll hear from him."

"Can you see anything?"

"I'm not a specialist I'm afraid so I just wouldn't be able to tell. You'll hear from Dr Ran soon enough."

***

Dr Ran held up the cross-section scans of the inside of his head as he entered, laid them out on the table between them.

"All clear - no problems except the wear and tear we'd expect at your age," he said, trailing a pen point over Kendal's brain. "But if you are still worried in, say, a year, go back to your doctor and he'll put you through again."

The Ran smile intensified. Kendal was about to say he would if he remembered to do so, but stopped himself and said a simple "thanks". His brains went back into a large brown envelope and they shook hands and parted. But if he'd thought that was an end to forgetfulness, alas it was not.

***

Kendal, huddled now against the worsening weather, is more confident than most about laying out a dead bait to achieve his objective. That is, he has chosen a dead fish over a live fish, or against other methods, including the plug lure he had trailed on the way to this spot and countless other spinning and glittering offers that either intrigued or annoyed pike to the point that

55

they couldn't resist making a strike.

As little as twenty years ago, livebaiting was the most popular way to fish for pike: a hapless roach or bream, not to mention the infamous ruffe, wrapped in wire and treble hooks and set to dangle, jiggling captives beneath an enormous cork bung.

Alfred Jardine, more than a century ago, had invented the livebaiting hook arrangement, which he patented - the Jardine Snap Tackle. A prodigious pike fisherman, Jardine nevertheless earned a reputation as a bit of a fibber: whenever a big pike was reported to *Fishing Gazette*, the angler's *vade mecum* of the day, old Jardine would pop out, there and then, and nobble one just a little better. *Fishing Gazette*, incidentally, was among the first magazines to add giveaways as an attraction to readers, among them the egg-shaped cork bung, still in use today, which comes complete with a wooden peg that fits tightly in the hole drilled through its core. With it, the line can be trapped to fish your livebait at any depth you chose. To this day, such floats are still known as 'Fishing Gazette' bungs. One of around the size of a small hen's egg was the most popular size for fishing livebaits, although massive floats of goose-egg size were available for fishing bigger livebaits: one had to match the size of the bung with the strength of the bait; while it can be allowed to bob and skitter over the surface it should not be pulled completely under by anything but the pike you are after. Even small pike seem unaware of the added resistance of towing a bung under the surface, at least until it's too late.

Although there were more humane ways of presenting a livebait - a single large hook through its tough and gristly upper lip, for example, livebaiting in all its forms is essentially cruel, Kendal thinks. He abandoned it years ago. Presumably many other anglers think the same because livebaiting is not nearly so widely practised today and is even banned on some waters.

Of the spinning and glittering objects that can be used to catch pike and other predatory fish, Kendal had a liking for the floating-and-diving plug. It had the huge advantage that it would float to the surface once you stopped pulling it through the water, and so could be navigated gently over weed beds and, by reason of the angled scoop beneath its chin, be made to dive into any weed-free holes between the beds by stepping up the speed again. He's used this method to catch many pike, although it's entirely non-selective - you are just as likely to catch a small fish as you are a big one, and as for really big ones...well, Kendal is sure he has that taped with the method he is now using.

He also has with him several spinners - spoon-shaped metal lures of various sizes that twist in the water. The vibrations these make are, in the right place, extremely attractive, and the confusion of glittering reflected lights that they throw off as the pike makes its final approach obscure the fact that it is closing on a mouthful of metal rather than a juicy fish. He uses these less and less, however, but does occasionally fish his dead baits using a method called trolling - trailing a bait that is mounted head-first (rather than tail-first as now) behind a boat. It's particularly useful for fishing in the often very productive areas just off marginal weed where pike hunt. It is also useful for searching for a catch in large areas of water. The bait can be raised and lowered attractively by changing the boat speed or raising and lowering the tip of the fishing rod, making it look like an injured fish. He has promised himself he will use this method for at least one day during his current fishing session if the still deadbaits are not very effective.

Kendal has so far not tried fly fishing for pike, 'flies' in this instance being large lures made from coloured feathers and not at all like the delicate creations used by trout fishermen to imitate natural flies. What they look like would appear to be immaterial, for they are reasonably effective as lures, particularly in America where they take not only large pike but also its close relative, the mighty muskelunge. However Kendal does know pike are extremely inquisitive and in the right mood will have a go at anything. Once in his younger days, while he was fishing for roach in a quiet canal winding-pool where narrow-boats are turned about, a pike entered the swim and set everything else dashing for cover. He had tied the only silver thing he could find at that time to his line - a drink-can ring-pull - and in no time at all hooked a leaping, tail-walking seven-pounder which had strained his light line to the limit.

***

His boat is now starting to buck more strongly on its anchor-rope as it twists in the teeth of a rising wind. The dinghy is the only comparatively recent addition Kendal has made to his pike-fishing repertoire. While he is quite sure it gives him a big advantage in this situation, he knows big pike can also be caught from the bankside. He's done it himself. But overall the boat was a wise choice, even if he's starting to feel more than a little exposed and vulnerable to the unpredictable strength of the storm which is undoubtedly poised to hit the loch.

***

When the powan disappeared Lucie had to move on. She had finished spawning and the hunger pangs had started to gnaw. Should she go back to the deep, just in case everything had taken a turn for the better? Although she had maintained her weight and even added to it slightly in the last couple of years in the abyss, it had been difficult to compete for the dwindling stocks of obliging little silver fish. At the time she'd left the deeps in order to spawn, it had become a desperately fierce place, where you had to keep looking over

57

your shoulder - and to look directly behind itself, a pike has to execute a total about-turn. She did not meet any pike larger than herself, but she did, from time to time, find very big fish dead on the bottom, clearly the losers of a fight (and alas too big to swallow). She could have quelled most adversaries, but the chance of becoming fatally wounded herself in the process was high. Instinct told her to avoid battle. And as for the powan, they'd become very scarce indeed; hard to find and uncharacteristically wary. She opted to stay away for a while and see how she could make out without a return to the increasingly unproductive chasm.

But even in her 'home' shallows, Lucie started to find life was not so rosy. It was not that there was any scarcity of prey fish; snack-size ruffe were now brilliantly abundant in addition to the roach, rudd and dace that had always been her mainstay in her younger years. But her own size, she found, made her that much more conspicuous and consequently avoidable, and it was also a large body to maintain, let alone making it even larger; her food needs had grown in proportion to her size, at least while she was still growing . She was very, very big, long and deep; small fish dived into weed and rushes as she approached, and stayed there to watch as the long, slab-sided green and gold monster slid past. She was also slower. It took real effort to accelerate her mass and although she could make kills, there were fewer of them and a lot of energy was being used in the process. As a result of all this she was constantly hungry, and although she was beginning to regain condition she was hardly putting on weight. Though she did not know it, if this catch level was not improved by the time autumn came around, she would find that preparing her body for the next spring's spawning would mean the sacrifice of some of her bulk. However, she was soon to make another very important, not to mention fortunate, discovery about her loch.

It turned out to be a long, dry summer, warming the vast lake considerably. The rivers that fed into it were low, their flow feeble, and what was more the shallows were drying out rapidly leaving Lucie a much smaller area of weed in which to hunt for rations. Even though that meant her prey had less cover to hide in, she was now so obvious in open water that only the very unwary did not find her threatening and turn tail. Skirting wider and wider into open water on her hunts, she one day came, completely unexpectedly, upon a large gathering of fish. They were salmon and sea-trout, which for some time had been running in from the sea in small groups in the expectation of reaching upriver spawning grounds. Here they'd had to stop, ambitions thwarted by the drought. Low flow in the loch's feeder rivers made running on up an impossible task, with barely a couple of inches of water in the riffles between the deeper pools of the river, while the upper rapids were a dangerous jumble of rocks with very little water in between the stones. With good rain and a decent amount of water swelling the river once again, even the larger salmon - and some of them were very big - would have been able to sail over these obstacles. For the time being all save a few of the smaller sea-trout were well and truly stuck.

All the while they were held back, their biological clocks were ticking. Ripe with ova and milt, they had taken on the coloration of fish already starting to spawn. The females had lost their bright silvers and had become black-backed and dull grey, while the males had grown lean and red-brown, with jutting hooked lower jaws that would serve them well trying to dig in the gravel alongside a suitable female and face-off any opposition. They had stopped feeding when they encountered fresh water. Now, aware they had to retain some of their energy to achieve their ultimate goal, they had scaled activity back to a minimum but would now and then rise and flop half-heartedly on the surface out of sheer frustration.

Once it rained and the game was on again, heedless of any risks and moving by night or on a dull day for preference, they would fling themselves over all barriers in a race to the clean streamy gravel beds of the upper river, dig troughs in the gravel runs and lay and fertilise eggs until they were all but spent. As a final gift to the future they would use the last of their energy to waft gravel loosely over the eggs to save them from being gobbled up by greedy little trout and other small fish. They would then abandon themselves to the flow, dropping further and further downstream while fresh-run fish just in from the sea rushed on past, caught up in the same drive for procreation. The new aim of the spent fish, now called 'kelts', was to regain the sea, feed again, restore condition and, in due time, make the spawning run again. Alas few would make it, a huge percentage dying before they even reached the loch let alone the sea. Foxes, seagulls, ravens and hooded crows would feast on their emaciated bodies beached at the waterside (the birds invariably choosing the eyes for a starter treat even if the 'corpse' still showed signs of life).

**

The gathering that Lucie came upon could hardly be termed a shoal since the salmon were not packed closely together but spread out over a wide area. Nevertheless, the whole mass did have a shape: it was like a pear, with the stem end, where there were the largest fish, pointing towards the river mouth. These were preoccupied fish, she soon found out, and while some were just too big to contemplate for a meal (pike not evolving any sort of technique for chopping up their dinner), she found she could pick off smaller fish at the fringes with ease.

In that particular year, the drought was a godsend. When the weather finally broke in the autumn she had really started to gain weight again on a diet of oil-rich, egg-packed salmon. But there was more to come. A little while after the first run had streamed up into the rising river, returning kelts started to appear. While some were barely more than a bag of bones they were easy to catch, and anyway her formidable digestive juices could easily break down scales, bone and gristle. A lot went into her maw, living and dead, with large numbers of kelts washing into the loch whenever there was a biggish spate.

While the feeding in her new situation was variable - feast to famine and back again all through the winter - it was not only sustaining but also adding more ounces from time to time. And after spawning in the following spring, Lucie sought out a good lie near the river mouth that would allow her to take full advantage of her new-found food supply while at the same time being not too far from the shallows as an alternative larder. A larder she is now scanning while the storm gathers all its forces. But bad weather is of no concern to her, save that it might bring down a few more kelts.

***

Her new modus operandi has not been without its risks, nor has it left her without scars; as with Kendal, the passing of the years has left its mark.

She finds herself more often than not in shallow water after the powan feasts dried up. This means she is frequently checked out from above by the newly-resident ospreys, who inevitably retreat, lofting away, when they realise her vast weight is considerably beyond their lifting capacity. Other large pike - and there are more than a few of them in this loch, but so far as she knows none bigger than her - are also occasional challengers for her territory, but she sees to it that they quickly realise this is no place to wait around. Otters are another matter altogether; her left pectoral fin, or rather the stump of it, gives a twinge every now and then to remind her of one particular encounter.

Chapter 9

It was a warm, summer afternoon, the sun giving the plankton-rich water an amber, dusty glow. She was moving cautiously...there was prey ahead. Three large roach, silver plated, red-finned, were feeding, preoccupied, in a pool of clear water hedged by weed. They did not need to root in the bottom or make a dash to catch the fat little damselfly larvae that were popping out of the mud beneath them and shooting, torpedo-like, for the surface in order to hatch into winged flies. All they had to do was pick them off one by one as they rose past them, or nose up to the surface to suck in those that got by.

Slowly, ever so slowly, Lucie manoeuvred herself into a position to strike from behind a flimsy curtain of weed. The roach were oblivious to her presence, intent on the easy feeding they had discovered, and she fastened her eyes on the best prize, the largest fish of the three - a handsome fellow bulky enough to keep her appetite satisfied for the rest of the day.

As he rose to intercept one more of the fat little larvae just before it reached the surface, she struck - only to realise at the last moment that something was hurtling towards her from the left, jaws wide open, its eyes on the same prize. It was a huge dog otter.

Lucie got there first. Her jaws clamped on the roach; in spite of the challenge she was determined to have her meal. But then there was a sudden stab of pain in her side. Although he was not much more than half her length overall, the otter had attacked. It would be hard to imagine what had made it round on this huge fish - perhaps it was miffed at having its prey stolen from under its nose - but attack it did, clamping its fangs shut on the largest appendage in its field of vision, which at that moment happened to be Lucie's pectoral fin, or rather the root of it. Lucie immediately recalled the otter that had hunted her in her youth, and was aware of the dangers the animal now posed.

The fin proved a lucky purchase for the otter. After spitting out the roach to attend to her own defence Lucie found herself unable to turn on the animal so long as it hung on to her. She twisted again, then tried a headlong dash along a pallisade of bankside reeds in an effort to brush her attacker off. But it stuck to her grimly: wherever she went, he went, whenever she turned, he turned with her. It was as if he had become some new limb she had suddenly grown. It was a painful extension, come to that, and she was bleeding too, leaving a dark trail through the water. Whenever she stopped swimming, it would start to claw at her with its huge, sharp-nailed webbed feet, and always it kept trying to pull her up, up to the surface.

Soon she became desperate, sensing that this was a battle she might actually lose: it could be a fight to the death. And in her desperation she remembered one vital thing about otters and other land creatures, something that just might save her: they could not live for long without breathing air. As a last resort she began trying to haul herself and the otter towards deeper water where she could hold it down until it either let go or drowned.

It was a good call but not an easy fight. Twice the otter managed to take her within a foot or two of the surface, using the whole of its sinuous body as well as its broad paddles and strong tail to exert force. But, bit by bit, she was making her way out of the shallows, towards the deeper water of the channel, pushing and pushing with all the strength she could muster to keep him down. And although at first it seemed that nothing would deter the vengeful creature, she eventually detected a weakening of his efforts. Was she winning? With every passing minute, it seemed, there was less force in his kicks, and a slackening of his hold on her side. But she was also growing weak from her efforts and loss of blood, and the pain was fierce.

If she failed, she would not be the first big pike to be found beached, dead at the side of the loch, with its soft belly and vitals eaten out by an otter. At last she felt the flow of the current and knew that there was seven or eight feet of water beneath them. Mustering the last of her strength she made a final thrust towards the bottom.

Five minutes is about the limit for an otter to hold its breath. Considering it had already closed its nose and ears in preparation as it struck at the roach, Lucie's assailant had now exceeded that time by a considerable amount. Now it was the otter's turn to feel desperate. It seemed it hadn't been such a good idea after all to attack this huge fish. As the bottom of the channel grew nearer and nearer, it was clear the game was up. It let go.

As Lucie sank gratefully to the bed she watched the big animal spiralling towards the surface. It looked lifeless, too tired even to kick, a few bubbles still escaping from its thick coat. Between them, in mid-water, floated a large transparent piece of Lucie's pectoral fin. Reaching the top, its head breaking though, the otter gave a deep gasp, then lay flat there in the open air for some time, waiting for strength to return before slowly paddling away. At least it was undamaged. Not like her.

Every bit of physical intrusion that penetrates the protective mucus covering of a fish's body can be life-threatening if the normally abundant fungal spores in freshwater gain a foothold, while deeper incisions, like the gashes made by the big-headed otter's massive teeth, could easily admit other infections. Blood-loss could be similarly dangerous, but fortunately in Lucie's case her wounds missed the main blood-carriers. Capilliary-leakage soon stopped, mercifully.

She was however deeply shocked that her assumed sense of impregnability had been shattered. But, as with all fish, this shock quickly dissipated once it was clear there was no longer a major external threat. To have any chance of survival in the continuous chain of predation in the underwater world, even a damaged fish must quickly get on with the business of living and put trauma behind them. Thus she felt the drive of hunger even though a large part of her very useful left pectoral fin had been ripped away. Luckily, although it was damaged, most of the heel-like driver muscle's stump remained and could even be moved gently, despite still hurting a lot. In time, though she was not to know this, some rudimentary fin rays and the delicate web that would join them even regenerated - but not perfectly. It would always now be a poor thing, rudimentary, half the area of the magnificent fan-like original. But, hungry as she was, her energy could not be restored as quickly as her appetite demanded.

For two days she skulked listlessly at the bottom where she had come to rest after her epic battle, fasting, denying her gnawing hunger while tissue and nerve cells knitted themselves back together and the pain abated. An angry red swelling, many scales missing, surrounded the damaged fin, and here and there were flecks of an opportunist white fungus trying to take hold. But by and by she could no longer put off feeding. She made her way to the shallows and without a lot of trouble was able to snatch a few unwary small ruffe and a couple of gudgeon, insignificant and unsubstantial fish that she would normally disdain. Over the next few days she added frogs to this menu. It wasn't a diet that would put on any weight but it was sustaining while she struggled to restore something that had gone oddly awry - her equilibrium. Without a port flapper, she was madly off-balance, veering this way and that to compensate for the propulsive effect of her still-powerful right pectoral fin. The other function of these fins was to adjust her trim, fine-tune everything ready for a strike, and because it took some time to adapt herself to her new dynamics she did not feel sure enough of her abilities to go after bigger, swifter prey. Not for some time, anyway. When she eventually managed a successful dash and kill, she did so with an odd corkscrew wobble that would remain with her for the rest of her life.

At least she was fully-functional again. Her formidable immune system, necessary for any fish that lives by continuously going into battle, had seen off any infection that might have got in through the initial injuries, while the fungus had been successfully stifled by mucus cells regenerating together with tough scar tissue.

**

In the increasing blast and chop Kendal smiles wryly as he remembers that he owns a high-viz orange buoyancy collar to go round his neck, bright as the painted tip of his float; were it not for the fact that it is in the storage compartment under his bed back in the van, it could prove a lifesaver if he should get tipped into the water! At least he has the old aluminium saucepan he uses as a baler in the bottom of the boat, at the ready in case too much rainwater and wave slops build up. For the moment, things are far from severe, and while the question of safety has momentarily crossed his mind he is content to dismiss it and settle back. Perhaps the stir will improve his luck, he tells himself, waiting and watching.

While he has always been a pike fisherman since his early experiences at Brightwell lake, it is not the only kind of fishing he has enjoyed. He has fished through the night for lake carp, deep, powerful and hard to tempt fish, and he's reached the waterside on many a summer morning to fish for olive-golden ruby-eyed tench as pink dawn creeps into the sky. And in the spring, he's enjoyed fly-fishing for trout both on rivers and in lakes and reservoirs. But he's always come back to hunting the waterwolf, and over the years, apart from his recent woes, the mission has taken up more and more of his fishing time. His current belief that he is on the right track for something spectacular is based not only on his own observations and thoughts but also on reading much of the pike-lore that has gone before.

He knows not when people first started fishing for pleasure, but he does see that fish must have been on the dinner menu since very primitive times, and that pike are one of the more palatable and easy to find freshwater fish. Relatively easy to catch, too, by reason of their enormous appetite which some might interpret as sheer greed. And they're usually pretty big - catching one must often have provided a feast for many.

He also knows that by the time *The Treatyse on Fysshynge with An Angle* was written in the mid-to-late 1400s (attributed to Dame Juliana Berners, prioress of St Albans, although her authorship is disputed by some) fishing with a rod and line is regarded as a sport, pastime, hobby, call it what you will, on a par with hunting and hawking. The good prioress prefaces her work with a theory that good sport and honest games lead to happiness and long life, and goes on to say that of the four 'good sports' hunting, hawking, fishing and fowling, fishing is the one that really floats her boat.

Of the pike, she says it is a good fish but she loves it less because of its inclination to eat those of its own kind. For baits she recommends fresh herring (she does not have the benefit of a freezer), a live roach or a frog, but recommends as a good wheeze tying a baited line to a goose's foot and sending the bird out on the water so that she can watch the resultant tussle between bird and pike. Something to remember for slow days on the riverbank.

Two centuries later, Izaac Walton in the more widely-known *Compleat Angler* is better on pike lore, although his assumption that pike are generated from water weed shows his natural history to be a little suspect: "*It is not to be doubted but that they are bred, some by generation and some not, as namely, of a weed called pickerel weed, unless learned Gesner be much mistaken, for he says this weed and other glutinous matter, with the help of the sun's heat, in some particular months, and in some ponds apted for it by nature, do become pikes.*"

Walton is a great gossip and likes nothing better than repeating whatever anybody tells him no matter how unlikely the story. His passage on pike is a wonderful collection of tall tales and has prompted later editors to add many of their own - it's worth reading again and again. But for more accurate observations on natural history, as well as stern criticism of some of the rubbish that has gone before, turn to the writers of the following three centuries!

Absorbing and useful as reading all this background material is, Kendal knows none of it compares to the real thing: breathless waits for a jiggling float to dive under (sometimes, if the strike from a pike is hard and fast, there's an audible 'plop!'), or a heavy thump on the line as a trailed bait or lure is grabbed. But what unknowing observers won't have seen is the preparation that has gone into any pike fishing campaign, choosing the bait or lure, finding the right spot, using the mind's eye to visualise what is happening in the watery world beyond the vision-obscuring reflections on its surface. It has all been bought together: now it's up to the pike!

Like many pike fishermen, Kendal concentrates his campaigns on the autumn, when the water weed starts dying back, and the following winter months, November, December, January and early February, often the coldest parts of the year when fingers numb and turn blue and ice forms in the fishing rod's guide rings. That's when pike are at their biggest, fittest and hungriest.

***

Kendal first met Alastair Sutherland on his initial trip to the loch a year earlier, coming upon him shortly after the pleasant surprise of finding the hotel so hospitable about keeping his van on the car park and looking after his frozen bait. Not that there were all that many people needing space there at the back end of the year apart from the odd birthday party and a dwindling number of wedding receptions. On these occasions the locals went wholeheartedly Scottish and the car park was full of big, loud men in tartan kilts, red-faced from drink and the excitement of it all, while the women tripped around them in high spirits and their best gowns.

These events often went on all day and even from his faraway spot out on the loch, noise of the merriment often reached Kendal on a calm day. Sound travels far and fast over level water, especially when aided by the amphitheatre acoustics of the surrounding hills. Returning from a day's fishing when one of these shindigs had died down Kendal saw a lone figure in a wheelchair parked on the semi-circle of sand - a wedding guest, obviously. Drawing closer, he noticed the man was in Highland dress, and he gave him a small boatman's wave - reciprocated - before shipping his oars and letting the dinghy glide into the alders at the edge of the bay. The invalid wheeled himself over and watched silently while Kendal tied up and unpacked.

"Pike fishing eh?" He said, looking at the gear when Kendal had put everything ashore.

"Why, yes," Kendal replied - a little surprised, for not everyone knew the different types of rod and other clobber used to catch different kinds of fish.

"And have ye had any luck?"

"A few," says Kendal, turning his attention to the figure who, he notices, is a little unkempt for a wedding guest, with straggly dark hair and bushy eyebrows adding to his wild appearance. "One around 25, and a couple just below 20."

"So you've seen no sign of the big one?"

The statement had pulsed through him like an electric shock. Even the memory of it still had the same effect. It was the first confirmation that he really was on the right track. His surprise must have been ovbious.

"Ay. There's a fush so big out there nobody will swim in this part of the loch. Ask anyone."

Kendal has heard the same story, or something like it, a million times: a pike that swallowed a whole goose in such and such a lake, one that jumped half out of the water to catch a horse by the nose and tried to pull it in, one that bit Billy Jones' leg off...monsters all. But this time, this time...this time it feels different. But since he has narrowed down his search to this place and this time, is this just wishful thinking?

"Really?" he says, tempering his enthusiasm with caution.

"Oh yes," says the Scotsman quietly and with conviction, "I've seen it myself."

***

Eager to learn more, Kendal had shaken hands with the man and introduced himself.

"Sutherland. Alastair Sutherland," came the reply. "Or at least, what's left of him."

Kendal raised his eyebrows.

"Stroke...a damned stroke. That's what I get for serving my king and country in Northern Ireland and surviving through God knows what, a bloody stroke." He stopped, seeing a figure approaching from the hotel.

"Ah, here comes Jimmy."

Jimmy, Kendal was to learn later, was Alastair's 'minder'. The odd couple had formed an unlikely partnership following Alastair's stroke four years earlier, the unemployed local young man stepping in to help when a slow recovery had begun and the hospital thought Alastair might be able to live at home with suitable assistance. Since Alastair had no wife, or the means to employ a housekeeper, the hospital was reluctant to let him go until a note in the local shop window for a carer who would earn a modest salary plus board and lodging drew a response from Jimmy. And so Jimmy became not only Alastair's housekeeper but also his means of transport, and in time this had developed into an inseparable bond. He was also the only person who could bring Alastair out of his recurring spells of deep depression. Beer with whisky chasers was part of the medicine.

***

"That's it, Jock. They've cleared up the bar and all the wedding guests have gone. We can go over now."

The young man gave a nod to Kendal as he grabbed the handles of the wheelchair and turned Alastair towards the hotel.

"Well, fisherman," said Alastair, looking over his shoulder. "Will you be joining us?"

It was an offer he could not refuse, so after stowing his gear and locking up the van he found himself with a pint in his hand listening to Alastair's story of the giant pike.

"Well, it was round about the end of June, I think, about a year ago, and we'd taken the bus round to the wee patch of grass where they picnic by the bridge over to the other side...it goes on to the village. Have you ever been there?"

Kendal shook his head. "No. Not so far."

"Do. There's a nice wee pub there I think you'll find to your liking. Anyway, there we are, perched up above the river, when along comes this little group of sea-trout. They're not quiet things like your brown trout, now, or steady like salmon. They splash about all over the place, like a pack of naughty schoolkids when the master's out of the room. You can hear them coming a mile off.

"I watch them rollicking away, up and under the bridge, when suddenly I notice there's this shadow moving up behind them. My first thought is it's three big salmon - you know the way they sometimes line up one behind the other, like geese - but then I nearly fall out of my chair. It's one fish...one big fish! And it's not a salmon at all but a pike. An enormous bloody pike, with a head so big..."

He held out his hands two feet apart.

"An' that's just the head, mind. The whole fish...why, it must have been six, seven feet long, maybe more. What sort of weight d'you think that would be?"

Again Kendal shakes his head. "No idea, not without a proper measurement. Enormous, though. And you saw it too?" He turned to Jimmy, who shrugged and looked embarrassed.

"Him see it? No. Jimmy was fast asleep in the grass dreaming of the games mistress round at the girls' school."

Jimmy laughed. "I don't know anything about pike," he said. "I'm a salmon man myself."

"What, the salmon here on the loch?" Kendal asked, interested, and in this case innocent of the fact he was rising to a bait.

"No, I get mine from the supermarket."

That was Jimmy, lightweight but likeable. Alastair Sutherland, however, had told his story with deadly seriousness, and his disclosure had given Kendal a thrill beyond words. Even with the human propensity to exaggerate wildly, particularly when it comes to the size of fish, a pike as long as three salmon has to be something extraordinary.

"And then?"

Alastair shrugged. "That's pretty much all there is to it. The sea-trout sailed on up under the bridge and over the first rapids on the other side which put them right out of reach. And I was about to wake Jimmy and show him but by that time the pike had started to drop back with the flow. But..." and he looked Kendal right in the eye, "It's as true as I'm standing here now."

"Sitting," Jimmy corrected him.

***

Alastair, Kendal had quickly learned, was one of the bar regulars. And as the weather worsened rapidly on that first trip to this particular part of the world, as was often the case at this time of year, the wheelchair-bound Scotsman was the mainstay of its trade and often the only customer taking advantage of the fireside. On most occasions Jimmy would find another pursuit once he had brought Alastair into the room. He was addicted to a group of pinball machines and one-armed-bandits in the foyer, and if anyone else of his own age was around they quickly ended up playing pool in the adjacent games room.

That brought Kendal and Alastair together quite often. Normally their convesations would strart with an inquiry about how the day's fishing had gone, but by degrees they got round to other topics and with the help of a few

68

drinks gently put the world to rights.

They'd talked too about Alastair's past. Inevitably, as a soldier on active duty, he'd lost close companions, and seen sights he could not even now bear to bring himself to talk about. Kendal knew when to dig no deeper; even journalists have an 'off' switch. And they'd talked too about Kendal's own life. The story of Mab's illness had affected the Scotsman deeply even though he did not know her and had never seen her except for the photo in Kendal's wallet he'd once been shown. He'd faced the same abyss as Kendal's wife, but by the grace of God he was pulling out of it, albeit slowly.

"You must be finding that very hard to take," he said. "I don't know that I could do it - she's there but she's not there."

At this point their eyes met and he saw deep understanding. The Scotsman reached out and put his hand gently on his shoulder.

"And you cannot even grieve, poor man."

The depth of that understanding was reassuring and uplifting to Kendal.

On clear days when he was out fishing, Kendal could usually see Alastair parked on the beach under the hotel scanning with a pair of binoculars for birds - his favourite pastime - and whatever else was on interest on the water.

"If I tell Jimmy I'm looking at the birds he just sniggers, the dirty wee man," he told Kendal, who in time noticed that Sutherland was not just a fair-weather 'twitcher' but dedicated enough to watch through all weathers, even storms when he would be wrapped in a vast yellow bicycle cape.

"Have you seen our ospreys?" he once asked, his voice full of pride that the birds had chosen his loch to nest.

"No. It's usually too late when I come up. They've already gone back to Africa."

"You'll have seen their nest, though?"

It could hardly be avoided - a vast pile of twigs on the top of a lone, tall pine on a rocky mid-loch island.

"I have," replied Kendal, "and I'm sorry I missed them."

On his autumn trips he was also too late to catch the other summer birds, the water-skimming swallows and martins and the swifts screaming as they spiralled into the warm summer night sky to spend all the dark hours on the wing, endlessly circling - true creatures of the sky which, but for the necessities of breeding, would abandon land completely.

He could talk birds with Alastair endlessly. If he'd missed the summer birds there was always the consolation of migrant birds from the far north, Siberia and beyond, winging in to spend the winter in these more hospitable climes. Storms in the Atlantic or the North Sea brought seabirds in to the more sheltered waters of the loch, even once a sea eagle from North West Scotland.

Golden eagles were commoner, but far harder to see when they dropped below the skyline and were no longer silhouetted. Comparing notes with the knowledgeable birdwatcher was a treat Kendal often found himself looking forward to.

***

Shortly after hearing Alastair's big pike story for the first time, Kendal had taken a day off fishing to make a pilgrimage to the churchyard in Kells, Dumfriess, where there is a stone memorial to one John Murray, gamekeeper. Kendal ran his fingers over the relief carving of a gun, a dog, a fishing rod and a partridge, and recalled the legend that in the late 1700s, fishing with a fly in Loch Kenn, the doughty retainer landed a pike all of 7ft in length and weighing a staggering 72lb, an unverifiable record only eclipsed by equally unverifiable reports of 90lb pike caught in Ireland. If both legends are true, he wondered on his way 'home' to the hotel car park, are pike getting smaller in terms of maximum size? It's an interesting thought, though not a new one to him, swiftly followed by a question, again not new: if they are indeed getting smaller, what might the reason or reasons be? In time, and without an answer, it's a question he stows away once again at the back of his mind. He prefers to think truly big pike are still around, and with Alastair's story, he's just had one of the clearest indications one is here, right under his nose. Unfortunately, in a few more days, the first of his newly revisited Hibernian forays is over.

***

However, today might be the day.

Of the two characters, Lucie and Kendal, steadily drawing closer to one another in the loch, threatened by a gathering storm, the pike is by far the most self-reliant. Although we try to see many of our fellow creatures in human terms and bestow on them some of our attributes, it is hard to imagine anything less worried about a lack of friendship - or the approaching bad weather for that matter - than Lucie. Since she was a tiny hatchling she has never regarded fellow pike or any other creature as a friend (nor they her, for that matter!). The affairs she has had have been biological necessities, with no hint of affection towards her partners. In fact, but for the circumstances in which they came together, she might well have eaten them so long as they weren't too big to swallow: she is hard wired to assess anything that moves in her world for its potential as food. In this impelling, single-minded quest she is relentless, determined. Not for nothing does the Normans' 'Lucie' belong on the escutcheons of the noble and brave - and the ruthless.

***

In no time at all, it seems to Lucie, she has swept the entire semi-circle of the shallows, the outward part of her patrol. And so far nothing - only vague hints of shoals of prime roach moving swiftly out of the way some distance ahead, and the odd passing gudgeon or ruffe she has once again come to regard as too small to be worth chasing. It is, she realises, coming to the end of the time when the formerly thick summer weed will hide her well enough to mount an ambush. It's the time of year when she should begin to switch to the river mouth and its migratory salmon and sea trout as a mainstay, and it is towards this area that she now makes her way. Despite a slow roll attributable to old injuries, her movement remains ghost-like, steady, stealthy. All to often, her target fish have been lulled into a false sense of security by the belief she is not moving at all, while every passing second brings her closer, closer...

Reaching the narrowing and shallowing neck of the river she eases herself out into the current, then drops and lies against the scoured-out bottom so that the flow over her back helps her to keep station with very little extra effort. Scanning ahead as far as her enormous eyes can see, she tastes the water. It has the flavours of mountain tops and far lofty crags she will never see, high heather moors, peat and roaming herds of deer, dust from a stone quarry, the bitter hint of petrol and tar road-wash, dying vegetation...and fish. And rain. The water from yesterday's downpours is still running off, while fresh rain now lashing into the topmost mountain streams has yet to reach this far. The fresh fish she can taste and smell went on up under the bridge and over the rapids in the dark on the back of last night's spate, but there are older fish, dying fish perhaps, still to come her way - kelts. Lucie hangs for a little while, trying to assess if any of these weakened fish are close. It does not appear so, and there's nothing in her field of vision even though this scour is often a good place for just-arrived fish and kelts alike to lie. Still, the storm that has just reached her could change all that, and help to flush kelts from their pools higher up the river. Which does not help her present hunger.

It grows darker. Rain is pelting the surface above her. Lightning suddenly flickers ahead, and the following rumble of thunder is almost overwhelming to her highly sensitive hearing. It spurs her to move, inclining her broad, paddle-like pectoral fins just enough to lift her gently away from the bottom. Slowly, she lets the current carry her gently backwards towards the deeper reaches of the loch, staying head-on to the stream so that invigorating oxygen-rich river water washes over her bright red gills.

***

Kendal is not normally afraid of thunderstorms but under these circumstances, as the only object jutting out of a lake being hammered metal-flat by the first onslaught of the rain, he feels more than a little exposed. What's more, he's wielding a fishing rod made of woven carbon fibres, one of the best conductors of electricity known to man. Nevertheless, with the rain beating down like this he has little choice but to pull the drawstring of his waterproof hood tighter and huddle as low as he can. He's heard tales of fishermen being fried in electric storms, so he's more than a little relieved when the wild and ragged grey weather front that delivered the lightning bolt moves swiftly on and strikes one black hillside some way behind him with a hefty crack, then another target further away still. The rumbles grow fainter and fainter. As the rain turns lighter he emerges from his huddle to take stock: within the few minutes that the storm's leading edge took to sweep past, it left three inches of icy water mixed with hailstones in the bottom of the dinghy. Everything else appears to have weathered it, so he sets to with gusto to bale out the bilges. Halfway through this energetic exercise he stops suddenly, alert but puzzled. What has made him stop?

Do fishermen have a sixth sense? Some will say they can tell you when fish are around without any obvious signs that this is the case, but there may be subtle pointers that they pick up on which don't actually look particularly significant. Small changes in water flow, perhaps, or hair-breadth movements on a fishing line which, even though the eyes have apparenly not registered them, have nevertheless been noticed by the more analytically acute brain. Or perhaps other factors are passing on the alert - a moorhen hestitating to cross a pool, a seagull turning to come back over the same stretch of river for another look, a shoal of tiny fish-fry suddenly scurrying for a weedbed, all noted subconsciously. This should not be confused with the very real fact that fishermen can and do 'read' the water itself more accurately than non-fishermen. Some of the signs they see on the water surface or interpret from the behaviour of other animals can seem insignificant to a layman.

Kendal has stopped with his arm extended, just about to tip a saucepanful of icy water back into the lake. Suspicious, he runs his eye over everything - the rod, the boat, the anchor, the line, his float, the dun cattle on the bank all lying with their broad and shaggy backs into the wind, the still-racing sky threatening yet more rain, the distant whitewashed walls of the hotel, cottages, a raven wheeling across the grey on the gale as if it was enjoying every minute...all appears well. He shakes his head and starts to bale again, but all the same the moment has left him uneasy, like a jumpy cat.

And it is cold, very cold, and growing colder by the minute. He peers intently at his float, beyond it. There it is again! Where there should be an even pattern, wave after wave rolling towards him, there's an almost indiscernable heave to the dark troughs between them in a line between his float and the river mouth beyond: a heave that is slowly but steadily moving towards him. He tenses further. Now he realises what has unsettled him, although what is causing the water movement remains a mystery. It could be a shoal of small fish, a big salmon, perhaps a kelt struggling to get back to the sea, a submerged clump of drifting weed, a waterlogged tree stump, even an otter. But then, while it is still beyond his float, the broken wave pattern stops, subsides. He holds his breath...is it a fish, and if it is, has it seen his bait?

**

Two feet above the grey loch bed and still moving gently backwards, Lucie passes the mackerel, running her giant unblinking eyes over the silver-white torpedo. She stops downsteam of it, halted more by its unfamiliarity than anything else. Although it's clearly a fish, it's unlike any she has ever seen, boldly striped with dark bars and apparently scaleless. It's also dead, or hasn't much time left if it's alive: she can sense no life-betraying electrical bursts, no flickers of movement are coming through her ultra-sensitive pressure sensors and its eyes have no life-brightness. She smells and tastes the essences washing towards her: if it is dead, at least it is fairly fresh. Oh well, a fish is a fish, and never being one to turn down the offer of a meal she inches forward, but carefully in case it still has a kick left in it.

**

Kendal has stopped baling out his boat and is now gripping his rod, aware that the movement he detected somewhere in the vicinity of his bait has not reappeared or moved on. It seems like an age has passed without any further sign of life - perhaps he was imagining it after all?

Then he holds his breath again - did the float move? He peers, willing it to go under. But instead, and to his puzzlement, it does the opposite, rising, falling over and starting to move slowly back towards the boat. A cascade of possibilities races through his head: a mass of weed has wrapped itself around his line and dislodged the bait so that the whole mass is being driven back to him by the current; ditto a cruising tree stump, or perhaps the fresh storm water surging out of the river is too strong for the bait to stay in place? The other possibility he dare not think about for the moment is that a pike has taken the mackerel and instead of heading off in a textbook dash that would set the float diving under the surface, it is heading straight back towards his boat. He faces a dilemma. If it is indeed a fish and he strikes immediately to set his hooks the pike might not have a proper hold on the bait, and it could be snatched straight out of its jaws; alternatively, if he delays for too long, his quarry might detect something suspicious like the drag of the line and spit the bait out. In a conventional attack the pike seizes its prey cross-wise in the jaws, and carries on for some distance with the momentum of the rush before pausing to move the meal into a head-first position so that it slips easily down the gullet. It is after the pause, when the bait has been turned, that the angler would normally give a sharp tug to set the hooks.

If it is a pike which is not playing by the rules, Kendal is thinking as the float continues to move steadily straight at the boat, there is another problem which all anglers will recognise...if you hook a fish that is moving towards you and cannot reel the line in fast enough to keep pressure on the hook-hold, you risk losing contact altogether. More fish are lost through having a slack line than for any other reason.

The float is quite close now and he decides to let it continue on its course, rising to his feet in the frail bobbing boat to guide the slack line round the anchor rope and to one side of the craft as he watches the orange torpedo pass straight under the hull and pop up on the other side, at the same time straining to see if he can make out what is hustling it along. Is that a shadow passing below, or just a trick of the light? He's unsure. The float cruises on, five yards, ten yards, fifteen...then it stops abruptly. Snagged, or what?

He has a lot of slack line out now, and he begins to recover it gently while the wind buffets his back and there's a sudden rattle of icy hail that momentarily flattens the stormy surface of the water. Now facing the other way, he can just about make out the tiny blob of yellow on the beach under the white hotel: Alastair is watching, but even with powerful binoculars he would probably be unable to understand the drama of the moment, let alone see much at all in this light. Kendal comes to the end of his slack line, pulling the wind blown arc of line straighter and straighter. He reaches a decision as the first small flakes of snow he has seen this side of summer start to flurry around him, disappearing in an instant as they hit the black water. He braces himself against falling over and lifts the rod sharply, striking. Time to find out what really is down there.

The whispering of his tautening line turns into a shrieking whine as the wind whistles around it. He has hooked enough pike in his time to realise straightaway that this is a fish, and a fairly solid fish at that.

***

Moving upstream to lie her head along one side of the bait, Lucie has twisted to pick it up and has drifted back under the shadow of the boat with the mackerel crosswise in her jaws. Beyond the boat, coming to rest in her own familiar lie, she is just in the act of turning her meal to swallow it when the fish she thought was dead gives an unexpected violent kick and she feels a sharp pain in the upper rim of the side of her scissor-like jaws. Oddly, with it has come a steady tug which seems to be trying to haul her upwards, towards the surface. Swinging sideways, she edges off her lie and starts to move in the opposite direction, letting the current push broadside on her huge flank to lend some assistance. It looks to her as if a flimsy single string of weed is attached to the mackerel and some other point upwards and ahead of her. By

74

rights these tactics should make it snap straightaway.

***

"Damn!"

Kendal's rod is arching alarmingly and he realises he has not slackened the reel drag enough to let his quarry draw line without threatening to break it. Fumbling, he twists the knurled tension screw on his reel with cold-numbed fingers, hoping he is twisting it the right way. If the rod reaches the limit of its curve, or if it is pulled down to point straight at the fish, all the force the fish is exerting will fall on the line and could stretch it beyond its tested breaking strain. Luckily the line starts to move away more easily with a steady, regular click from the dampening drag. Measuring the new less alarming curve of the rod, and the rate the line is unhurriedly paying out, he tries to imagine just what is happening down below.

"She's kiting," he tells himself aloud, now convinced he has hooked a pretty big pike which by definition will be a female. Could this be 'the' one? Hard to tell at this stage. He moves his rod to his right in order to change the direction of pressure - he doesn't want her to go on drifting like this, taking more and more line to a point where its sheer elasticity would make controlling the fish very difficult. He detects an annoyed shake of the head, but still the fish drifts on. Ratchet up the pressure perhaps? Taking hold of the line ahead of the reel between the thumb and index finger of his spare hand, a far more sensitive control than the mechanical drag on the reel, he pinches gently. The rod curves into a tighter arc again, but not for long - the taut line cuts suddenly sideways, pulling the rod-tip after it in a new direction. His fish has woken up!

Prepared, Kendal lays his rod over to one side to counter the dash.

"Well, hello my beauty," he says to himself, again out loud. "Looks like we have a battle on our hands."

Chapter 10

Whether or not Lucie remembers from a summer long ago the unhappy combination of boat, line and angler we shall never know. She does, however, sense that she is once again in danger. Her immediate reaction, when the line tightens for a second time and makes the pain in her jaw all the sharper, is to go all-out to fight against it. Her first thought is to head for the shallows and thrust a way into the security of the weed there, scant and flimsy though it is at this end of the year. She might also be able to use the stems to rub away whatever is biting into her mouth. She has managed to spit out the mackerel by this time but it is still attached, hanging outside her mouth. When she dashes forward it flaps backwards over one eye, much to her annoyance. But depite all her efforts, a relentless pressure prevents her from running to the weeds as quickly as she would have liked.

***

Kendal, on the other hand, prefers to contain the battle arena to open water. He has lost fish in weed before. He concentrates on slowing down the first mad rush, knowing there may be many rushes to follow. He also knows each succeeding run will be a little less powerful than the last one as the fish begins, hopefully, to tire. If he manages to stop his fish before she gets to the shallows, retrieve a little line before she sets off again, he might be out of danger and clear of any snags - bar one: he still has his anchor down, and an anchor rope or chain is often the saviour of a fish as it makes its last desperate lunge for freedom. For the moment, though, he has too much on his hands to give drawing it in more than a passing thought.

"She's slowing...she's slowing." Still he talks to himself, absorbed by the interrelationship with his quarry. There is more snow whirling around him now in tiny flakes - a sure sign this is more than just a passing shower of wet snow. She's a big fish, of this he has no doubt, because he can test the weight of her against his counter-pressure. As big as anything he has caught so far, that's for sure, well into the 30lb class and perhaps a lot more. At the same time there is also something odd about her otherwise steady pull, a sort of vague wobble which intrigues him. What could that be?

His task is nerve-wracking. At any moment the hook-hold could fail or some weakness in the line or in his knots could betray him. With the single-filament nylon line he is using, strength relies on its diameter: if it is pinched by a badly-tied knot while under pressure it can be considerably weaker that its advertised strength, in this instance a breaking strain of 15lb. Again, all risk of putting this to a severe test is lessened in open water where he can let the fish run again and again without being heavy-handed about putting on the brakes.

Thwarted just yards short of the weeds the fish changes tactics and makes a right-angle turn to run upstream, towards the river mouth. Kendal increases his pressure, tries to bring her round in a wide circle, but she ploughs steadily ahead in spite of his efforts. Kendal begins to sense the power of her, for his inability to make her turn her head whichever way he directs means only one thing: bulk. His conviction that he has now hooked not just a big fish but a massive one is growing with every minute. This belief is strengthened when she stops abruptly, just waits, immobile and apparently unmovable. The orange float bobs up even though the line is tight - she can't be very deep in the water. She's now ahead of him at about two o'clock and still a long way away. He can use the float to judge progress as tries to inch back line, slowly, painfully. It is like trying to haul in a large sack of potatoes. What's she doing - thinking?

His answer comes when the float dives abruptly in a new direction, taking another right-angle turn, this time headed across the bows of the boat but still a considerable way ahead. Kendal is able to gain line as she does this, winding furiously to take up the slack, keep up the pressure and maintain his hook-hold.

Reaching mid-channel she dives deep and veers upstream again. To Kendal this seems an unwise tactic on her part, for she now has the river current to fight besides him. However, he finds the resistance more even solid, with his quarry able to flatten herself against the bottom and use the pressure of the flow over her upper body to make her stick fast, again almost immovable. Nothing for it but to hang on grimly until she loses patience, he tells himself. Ten minutes, a quarter of an hour passes while he stands face-on to the blowing snow amid angry wavelets and long wind-lane slicks of blown, rusty foam, the taut line sometimes moaning and sometimes shrieking in the rise and fall of the gale. He's not to know it, but the warning has gone out for storm force ten around the rugged west coast; some of the buffets could well be bound inland to the loch.

And then, all at once, the line falls slack, taking him by surprise. He has a momentary glimpse of the float racing towards him before it disappears. She's off again, and this time she is running straight at the boat!

He has heard tales of hooked mako sharks turning on their would-be captors and hurling themselves into a fishing boat to wreak havoc, but never, so far as he knows, has there been an instance of angry pike doing likewise. Of more concern is the fact that his line is now slack plus, even if the hooks hold, the fish is heading straight for the anchor rope. It will either hit it or pass to the left or the right. Which? If he gets it wrong his line could easily be smashed. He takes a gamble and switches his rod as far out to the left as he can reach, with a 50-50 chance of success. With huge relief he watches as the zipping line whips past on that side of the boat and carries on behind, rapidly taking up the remaining slack.

She's now moving at a terrific rate and before all that energy slams into the rod he lessens the tension control so that she can carry on astern unchecked as far as he feels he can safely let her go, which is about 150 yards. She's built for short, sharp rushes, he knows, not sustained swimming at speed. When he again applies pressure the effect of the new angle of the line lifts her away from the loch bed and upwards. At the end of the dash he sees her wallowing on the angry surface and can get a measure of her for the first time. She is enormous. She is possibly the biggest pike anyone in memory has ever seen, with the exception, maybe, of Alastair Sutherland.

Just as anyone's terms of reference are challenged (at least in the subject of size) when, say, encountering a truly tall person, he's amazed, stunned, astonished, staggered all at once. But then she dives, reminding him there is work to be done, and he buckles to. But it's not without the thought coming into his head that he has not really planned what he might do if he actually wins so huge a fish.

While he still fears the anchor rope might prove a fatal snag there is absolutely no way Kendal can attend to it at the moment. At least the fish is now safely in open water and he can resume a war of steady attrition, drawing a little more line back after each of her steadily less forceful runs. Each time she nears the boat, sees him looming above, she renews her efforts and sails away again, six, seven times. Fighting the sheer mass of her is something he has never had to cope with before. It is, he knows, putting a severe strain on him and his skills as well as on his tackle. A 15lb breaking strain line seems woefully inadequate for the task, but miraculously it's holding out. He hopes - he prays - that she hasn't the strength or will to jump. He's had really big pike that suddenly launch themselves into the air and skitter for yards and yards across the surface by violently thrashing their tails. If they manage to throw all this force and weight directly against the bent rod there isn't a strong enough line in the world to stop them smashing it like cotton. Is she simply too big to get airborne, he wonders. It would take a lot of energy to hurl such a mass at the sky.

Luckily she doesn't jump, and at last, at long last - he does not know just how much time has passed - he senses the fight has gone out of her. All he now needs to do is ignore his aching arms and shivering legs and inch her gradually to the surface, bring her alongside. Then what? He's shocked that he hasn't given enough thought to this outcome so far. It will be a job - perhaps impossible - to get her into his landing net. Designed for large pike as it is, nothing like this fish ever entered the thoughts of its makers. Nevertheless he looks down into the boat for it, only to find to his utter dismay that he hasn't even remembered to unfold it or fix it to its pole!

He's unprepared also for just how long she is as he gently but firmly coaxes her upwards, desperately wondering how he is going to manage the next stage of the operation and cursing himself for not being well prepared. She's almost under the boat now, her stature growing as he can see more and more of her rising on her side through the murk. And suddenly, it seems, there she is, lying docilely alongside the boat, beaten, the one huge eye that he can see assessing the situation, a cold unblinking eye that he's sure is still calculating in terms he will never understand. His annoyance about his own unpreparedness is replaced by growing wonder - can she really be more than half the boat's length, and such a deep slab from her dark olive back to her pearly belly as she lies there, wallowing? And what's that...a curious, stumpy appendage waving at him where her pectoral fin should be? Some past injury has marred her otherwise perfect body. That explains the wobble! Now he can see the one treble hook that has a purchase in the upper side of her jaw, and the apparently undamaged mackerel still trailing from two more treble hooks outside her mouth. Now he can also see that she will not only break the pike record, but smash it by a considerable margin. But he's now reminded, as she makes a half-hearted thrust with her broad tail, that just a few problems lie in the way.

With one eye on the fish he sees that the landing net is just not up to the job, even if it were properly set up. Fortunately he has remembered to bring along a three-metre keepnet in case he needs to catch bait fish. He rules out another tube net he has with him that is designed for keeping large pike - it would make even a 50-pounder extremely uncomfortable, and besides there is no way of getting her into this while she is actually in the water. On the other hand, if he screws the landing net pole to the mouth of the keepnet, he wonders, will he be able to coax her into it? Certainly it's long enough and wide enough. That would solve a few problems if he could manage it.

If he wants to claim a record he has to produce the fish and have his catch witnessed, even if he does so with this beautiful creature as a dead body, which he'd certainly not wish to do. If he secures her in the keepnet and rows gently, he decides, he can tie up and find somebody, Alastair or Jimmy perhaps, to verify his claim before setting her free. To add to his woes, the scales he has somewhere in his tackle aboard the boat are simply not made to handle weights of more than 50lb and he's pretty sure she'll beat this by a mile, so finding something better to weigh her with is a prority too.

Of one thing he's very, very sure - she's not coming into the boat. Not only could she prove a muscular and dangerous companion to share his space with - her head is huge and her wickedly toothed jaws are enormous - but if he tries to haul her aboard on his own he runs the real risk of capsizing. Besides, she'd very quickly die out of the water, so that was definitely out even if he had the ability and strength to ship her in. For all its size and ferocity the pike is a species unable to live long out of its element, especially after it has given its all in a long fight.

Wet and cold and standing in a rocking boat in a storm does not make decisions easy. The keepnet is not the best of plans, but it is a plan. Holding the rod high with one hand so that he still keeps the line to the fish taut, he stoops to scoop up the landing net pole and push the screw-in socket at its end towards the screw fitting on the rim of the concertina-like keepnet's mouth. He nudges the fittings against each other. A couple of sharp turns with his wrist and the screw bites. So far so good. He's about to take another turn to secure it properly when his mobile phone rings. Lowering the pole and net into the boat, he feels under the waterproof flap of his breast pocket for it, and answers with a terse "Yes?"

"Dad?"

It's Jenny.

"Jenny, look, very busy...call you back five, ten minutes..."

He's about to put his thumb down to close the call when he catches the urgency of the little voice at the other end. He slowly brings it back to his ear.

"No, Dad, no, it won't wait. It's Mum, Dad. She's gone."

At first he misunderstands, wrenched away from his present predicament.

"Gone? Where?"

"Oh, Dad, I'm so, so sorry. She's dead. Oh Daddy, our lovely Mab's dead."

"You mean...?"

"Yes. Can you come right away? Where are you? What are you doing?"

Nothing has prepared him for this. Even the fact that he is in the middle of a broad loch in a snowstorm with a huge fish alongside has momentarily faded from his consciousness.

"I'm fishing. I'll call back when I get ashore, quickly as possible."

The fish is now the least of his concerns. He throws his head back. Though most of it is whipped away by the gale, the wail he directs at the sky makes the nearest bankside cow stumble suddenly to its feet and look at him with astonishment, pawing the ground and snorting out a cloud of steam. Its companions stir restlessly. Then he looks down, diverted by a movement in the water, and blinks with surprise and horror.

As if to compound his misery, the hook has pulled free and the enormous

80

pike is slowly, ever so slowly starting to drift away!

He tries to attend to the new challenge. It's a crisis that helps to temporarily blot out a more painful reality. But even as he thinks about picking up the pole and net again he can see that his prize is already drifting out of reach. The only rational thought that comes into his head is the fact he still has his phone in his hand and he can at least use its camera to catch an image of her. He puts his rod down, flicks the camera control on and raises the instrument as the mackerel bait, still attached to his line, sinks beneath the boat to leave only the float bobbing at the surface. He takes one, two, three pictures, trying to keep bits of the gunwale in focus to give some idea of the fish's sheer size. Then before his eyes, like someone recovering from a shock, the big fish realises she is untrammelled, rights herself and starts to sink slowly down into the black inky deeps behind the boat.

His misery doubles, the losses acute, his fingernails digging into his palms and a stream of tears clouding his vision. But then he has to squint, focus: to his astonishment the orange float riding idly behind the dinghy bobs once, twice, speeds up, then disappears with a plop. Surely not a second chance! She hasn't really taken the bait again, has she? He pockets the phone and reaches for the rod.

There's a fair bit of slack line to take up, but as soon as he feels resistance he strikes. It's a solid feeling and he can for a second or two believe he has hooked the big fish again. But this time it is not moving. And from the angle of the line he guesses what has happened - it has gone around the anchor rope. Has she gone under the boat again, perhaps, this time towards the river, and in the process tied herself up? A couple more tugs are useless. He puts the rod down and grabs the rope at the bows and starts to haul, hoping against hope to feel that enormous fish once again. It starts to come in. Good - there's something kicking there, too, but so far nothing that offers a lot of resistance.

But with two yards to go before the weighty iron wheel anchor itself comes up, all is revealed. It's a pike all right, but a bewildered-looking five-pound jack pike with the secondhand mackerel halfway down its throat. Dismayed, he hauls the last of it in, fish, bait, weight and all, and as he does so the jack violently regurgitates the bait and clonks down into the bottom of the boat where it wallows on its side in five inches of dirty, ice cold water, glaring defiantly up at him.

Is this all the consolation he can be offered? This miserable, unwanted creature that has intruded into his grief? Something infuriates and possesses him, drives his dismay towards the irrational. Though he has only ever killed a trout or two for supper, he stares down at the jack as if it is something evil and raises the iron wheel over his head while the freed boat lurches beneath him. Then he hurls it down at the wretched fish, and makes the sky ring with another wail of pain.

Too late, once he has loosed the missile, to realise that without the bottom boards he has promised his dinghy, a scant few millimetres of resin and glass won't stop the irresistable force of it. For just a few milliseconds, there's a patch of pitch-black water where the pike previously lay, his own reflection looking up at him with disbelief, and then, with a rush, water is flooding unstoppably into the boat while he stares, paralysed, shocked by his own folly. The half-flooded boat cants and he stumbles, sits heavily, grasps the gunwales, sinking with the boat, half submerged already, something clutching at his left ankle, drawing him down into the breathtakingly cold water along with the dinghy and all his tackle. He reaches down: the anchor rope has twisted itself about his leg. His fingers tear at the tightening loop but he cannot loosen it.

"Is this how it ends?" he says to himself as the water reaches his neck while he flails his arms and bitter cold draws the very last of his warmth away. It is, he thinks, a very odd view of the loch, sitting here in a submerged dinghy and anchored to the bottom with just his head barely above water. At eye level an oar floats into view and with his last ounce of strength he reaches out to clutch it. He remembers nothing else...

Chapter 11

Exhausted and certainly not feeling herself, Lucie has watched all this from her lie downstream of the drama. After sinking more than actually swimming here she saw the bait that had caused her so much trouble starting to tumble down towards her, only to be snapped up in mid-water by a little pike dashing in from nowhere (had she been in a fit state she would have been able to swallow him whole, plus the mackerel for added relish). Perhaps the jack had then noticed her presence and become aware of the danger: anyway, for whatever cause, it dashed upstream for all it was worth, only to snag the angler's line on the boat's anchor rope, come to an abrupt halt and jerk the iron anchor wheel with a puff of silt. Trapped, the little fish tried to dash off again, which merely made him swim round and round in ever-decreasing circles, knitting the line tighter and tighter round the rope. It was still tugging away furiously when the weight was hauled up towards the boat, finally disappearing through the ceiling of the loch surface. The wheel followed.

The freed boat had then started to gradually drift towards her on the current. This made her nervous, restless. She was just wondering whether she still had the strength to shift away in case it posed more danger when there was a tremendous crash which jarred her sensitive ears and her considerable array of pressure sensors. The anchor weight, with the little fish still attached to its rope, came hurtling back down again - this time through a jagged hole in the bottom of the boat. Miraculously the little pike zig-zagged slowly away, dazed but not very seriously hurt. Then the boat started to sink, bow-first, following the weight.

As it nosedived towards the bottom, twisting slightly, she could see the man was still in it, seemingly a part of the whole ensemble, struggling. She kept her unfeeling eyes on him as the struggles grew weaker.

He now dangles there, still lying upright in his boat which has come to rest vertically with its stern uppermost because of air trapped under the fibreglass back seat which is all one of a piece with the stern plate. The man's head is only just out of the water. There does not seem to be much life left in him, if any at all.

Chapter 12

Kendle may yet have a guardian angel. Alastair Sutherland has watched the unfolding emergency from the beach with his binoculars.

"Jimmy!"

His roar rings out and he strains to wheel himself as quickly as possible towards the hotel where he knows his minder is in the bar. Fortunately the younger man is just at that moment emerging to bring him a customary wee dram.

"Call 999. Now!" Sutherland bellows, gesticulating. Rushing up to stand in the middle of the road, Jimmy passes over the glass and snatches his mobile phone out of his pocket, dialling while Alastair sketches the situation.

"A helicopter. Hurry, man. We may already be too late," Alastair finishes, realising for the first time he is holding a glass of whisky and downing it in one go. Jimmy nods, and relays the request. Then he wheels Alastair hurriedly back to the beach to look out across the stormy water, both straining to see if there is any sign of the luckless fisherman.

What seems like an age passes, but then a scene that wouldn't be out of place in an action film unfolds: they can see the flashing lights of a police car making its way rapidly down the opposite mountainside road to the village on the edge of the loch. A finger of white wake then emerges from below the village: they've got a boat out. And moments later, climbing above the dark bulk of the hill, there's the air-sea rescue helicopter from RNAS Gannet coming to the rescue too. A spotlight stabs down from it as it checks, then swoops to leave the shore, throwing a racing circle of light on the water as it makes a beeline for Kendle.

"We've done what we can," Sutherland says to Jimmy, who nods soberly. The birdwatcher raises his binoculars again.

"There's ropes going down now. And they've put a man into the water too," he reports to his companion. "The boat's there as well. An' now they're winching the both of them up, looks like. All we can do is hope."

With a sudden deep roar from its engines the helicopter lifts and wheels away. They watch until it is out of sight and a white streak shows the police dinghy is well on its way back to the village.

"A drink, I think," says Alastair, lowering his binoculars. "We won't hear any more until it's on the news. I don't often say my prayers, but I think it might be appropriate now."

The snow has stopped but it's cold - bitterly cold. What it must have been like out there in the water the good Lord only knows.

***

The thunderous approach of the helicopter, shortly followed by the arrival of a rubber dinghy with a powerful outboard motor, drove Lucie off her patch, but she came to rest near enough to see another man drop from the sky and then dive underwater to check what was holding the fisherman. When he'd freed him, hacking at the rope with a knife, he had put a sort of harness round both of them and they suddenly disappeared skywards. The fisherman's boat, meanwhile, decided it was finally time to sink properly and lowered itself gently to the bottom a couple of yards ahead of Lucie's habitual lie. The rubber boat that had been circling headed away, back towards the village, while the helicopter engines roared again. But she kept her new position, though wary. A few seconds later the big machine rose and whirred away, the intense vibrations gradually dying. Soon everything was quiet again, although above the water the gale still buffeted the loch. It was almost dark when she sidled cautiously and painfully back to her lie.

***

"The fact he was so cold was hugely lucky."

The doctor at Glasgow Southern General is talking to Jenny about him. Talking as if he wasn't there, or as if he was some kind of pet which did not understand even simple language. But Kendal is getting used to this and he no longer minds so much: he is alive. That's what matters the most.

Apparently he had actually died, they had already told him that. It wasn't an experience he remembered later: so far as he knew there was no tunnel with a white light at the end, no old gent signing him into the exclusive celestial club or even the raging firestorms of hell, although he had recalled the story of a fisherman who thinks he has gone to heaven because every cast he makes produces a beautiful, perfect 3lb trout. After a whole day of this the fisherman is tired but happy and - he believes - in paradise. After a week of it, of course, he realises he is in the other place.

Kendal had drifted in and out of consciousness, unable to speak coherently while white-uniformed people moved busily about him. But he'd woken with an angel looking down at him: Jenny.

He'd realised for some time he was in hospital, but where it was actually located was another matter. And he remembered almost at the same time the moment of folly that had brought him here. And the fact that Jennie had phoned him just before all that happened.

"Jenny. Tell me about Mab."

It was the first time he had found his voice properly other than making monosyllabic requests for needs such as water. He had a headache and his eyes hurt, but it was good to see her. She stepped closer, put a warm hand on his cheek, bent and kissed him.

"It's all over, Daddy. And it wasn't bad for Mab. It was...it was very peaceful. In her sleep. You're not to worry. Everything is on hold until you come back. We just need to get you well."

"Where am I?"

"Glasgow. You must rest. There is nothing to worry about."

"But you need help. The baby..."

She held his arm, squeezed, smiled.

"Dad, it's all right. Mike came straight away. He's been a brick. I think he's going to stay. Look, here's the doctor now."

She stood. She was now being told about his rescue and revival while he listened in, an incidental third party. The doctor seemed glad the patient was talking and improving.

"It was touch and go really but as you can see we have him back. They managed to keep his vital functions ticking over in the helicopter despite once losing him. We kept his temperature down when we got him in and only raised it very, very slowly. There's always a risk of brain damage, you understand, from lack of oxygen to the brain - usually its daft small boys who've fallen through the ice. We'll do some more tests but I think we're past the worst. No obvious signs of anything to worry about so with luck and a bit of rest he'll recover fully. Does he always go out fishing in those conditions?"

Jenny does not answer the question, looks over the doctor's shoulder and gives Kendal a small wave. "Thanks. You've been wonderful, all of you," she says. "I don't know how to even start thanking you."

"He should take more care, perhaps," the doctor concludes, turning to give Kendal a nod and half-smile before moving on.

***

"I hope this doesn't mean you'll try to stop me going back there to fish again?"

He's with Jenny on the train south a few days later.

"Wouldn't dream of it," she says. "But give it a little time perhaps?"

***

"That's her."

The print from the downloaded image on Kendal's phone is blurred but it's clearly a big pike: just how big it would be hard to tell. He has placed the picture on the seat of a hotel chair so that Alastair can see it. Jimmy is craning his neck over Alastair's shoulder to get a glimpse too. It's a year later, and Kendal has made this trip especially to thank them for their part in his rescue. The hotel has been wonderful about letting the van stay while he was away,

86

even emptying the fridge of food and bait and disconnecting the gas after he posted them the door key.

"Aye, that's her all right."

"And I had her right up beside the boat, right up beside it. At least six feet, maybe more. That means at least sixty pounds, maybe more. Maybe a lot more."

Alastair looks up at him keenly. "Such a shame you couldn't claim a record."

Kendal is glad that neither Sutherland nor anyone else knows exactly what went on in the boat. It will remain with him forever but will never be disclosed. He has buried his wife and grief rolls over him in overwhelming waves at times, like deep, despairing notes drawn from a cello; perhaps it always will, but he can feel within himself a need to move on, even if it's more a matter of determination rather than conviction. On the bright side, either his memory is improving or he's become less worried about its shortcomings. And from time to time he can smile. He does so now.

"I caught her. That's all that seems to matter."

"Aye. And you'll be out after her again, no doubt? She'll be waiting."

Another smile.

"Maybe next year."

***

A fully recovered Lucie now has the shell of a boat as extra cover to ambush the more active kelts that come her way. It may well stay there long beyond her span, like the boatful of petrified warriors at the other end of the loch. In pike years, she's probably already endured longer than she might but as yet she remains active and does not display the saddest sign of aging that can afflict a pike: loss of teeth. Many of her kind have to spend their declining years scooping up carrion through gummy jaws, unable to pursue or even hold onto active prey.

In time, one of her own genetically-endowed offspring might take her place. Perhaps some of them, like her, are already huge and will be similarly long-lived. But don't imagine for one moment that this large, aged, cold-blooded and empty-stomach-motivated creature in her alien underwater world has any human attributes other than the name we have given her: Lucie.

THE END

Lightning Source UK Ltd.
Milton Keynes UK
UKOW05f0336021216

289050UK00021B/1046/P